# THE MYSTERY OF THE NEBULOUS NEMESIS

# THE THREE INVESTIGATORS

## IN

# THE MYSTERY OF THE NEBULOUS NEMESIS

BY

## ELIZABETH ARTHUR & STEVEN BAUER

BASED ON CHARACTERS
CREATED BY ROBERT ARTHUR

Hollow Tree Press 2026

A HOLLOW TREE PRESS BOOK

Copyright © 2025
Elizabeth Arthur and Steven Bauer
Hollow Tree Press LLC

Jacket Concept Elizabeth Arthur
Jacket Design and Cover Art
© 2025 Hollow Tree Press LLC
Cover Art Pashur House

"The Three Investigators" ® & "???" ®
By Permission of Elizabeth Arthur

Published in the United States of America
All Rights Reserved



ISBN PB: 978-1-965321-39-3
ISBN HC: 978-1-965321-40-9
ISBN EB: 978-1-965321-41-6

# CONTENTS

1

## Trouble in Bakersfield

**"W**atch out!" a man yelled, his voice tense and strident. "Quentin, for god's sake, hold steady!"

Pete Crenshaw and Bob Andrews had just turned the corner onto Rocky Beach's Main Street when Pete stopped short. Halfway up the block a black upright piano hung ten feet in the air, held by three thick ropes attached to a bulky block and tackle. On the sidewalk, two men and a teenage boy held fast to the ropes, straining against the weight. The man had been yelling at the boy who looked uncertain and a little afraid.

In just an hour Pete and Bob were due to join their friends Jupiter Jones and Mallory MacLeod at HQ2, their new Three Investigators Headquarters, and they'd already run into several unexpected delays. Now here was another one.

It was early afternoon in Rocky Beach, and Pete had volunteered to help Bob pick out a surprise present for his father, Malcolm Andrews. Although Pete thought they'd allowed plenty of time to search for a good present, they certainly hadn't expected to run into this. He and Bob had left their bikes in a rack at the edge of downtown.

At the Salvage Yard, The Three Investigators and Mallory were not only supposed to discuss a possible new case, but also to give their friends Wally Tate, Isabella Chang, and Charlotte Mitchell a tour of HQ2. Now – ahead of where Pete and Bob were caught up in a large crowd – a gray truck with ANDERSON MOVERS on its side in large red letters was taking up one whole lane. Cars were backed up in both directions. The piano tilted to the right.

"Whoa!" Pete said. "I guess the stairs were too narrow." Bob nodded and they both craned their necks. Pete could see that the piano's ultimate destination was a tall open window in the second floor loft where another man's head appeared. That man was attempting to steady the block and tackle with another rope.

"Quentin!" the man on the sidewalk said, a little less loudly this time. "Straighten up, son!"

Pete could see that the teenage boy was shifting from foot to foot uncertainly, when he should have been solidly rooted. He leaned his head as far to the left as he could and swiped his chin on his shoulder. "O.K., O.K.," he said plaintively.

"This doesn't look real safe," Bob said.

"You can say that again," said Pete. "Does that kid know what he's doing?"

"I don't think so," Bob said. "It looks like his father's decided to give him some on-the-job training."

"That's good, I guess," said Pete. "Though maybe he should have started earlier in the kid's life."

Since there was no reasonable way to keep walking toward Uncommon Treasures, a shop on Main Street that sold all sorts of cool stuff and that Pete had suggested might have a great gift for Bob's father, Pete and Bob stayed where they were. Bob wanted to buy his father something to make up for a mistake he'd made in the course of The Three Investigators' first case of the summer.

The mistake could have cost Bob's father his job as a journalist at the Los Angeles *Sun*, and though he hadn't blamed Bob in any way once he understood what had happened, Bob still felt bad about it, and Pete understood why. Bob and his father were tight and the last thing on earth Bob would have wanted was to cause his father trouble.

The piano swayed as the boy struggled to hoist his end of it higher, and Pete was relieved when the upright finally leveled out and settled down.

"Yikes!" Pete said. "That thing must weigh five hundred pounds."

Down Main Street, someone leaned on a horn. The traffic jam caused by the moving truck was getting worse and Pete could see that the man who'd been barking out instructions was feeling more and more tense.

"O.K.," he yelled. "Let's get this *done*. On three, we pull together. We only have about ten more feet to go. Are you ready, Charlie?"

He was calling up to the man positioned in the open window, ready to swing the piano sideways and into the room. Pete couldn't see, but he was sure there were at least two men up there.

"Ready," Charlie yelled.

"One, two – "

"Wait, wait, Dad!" Quentin yelled. "There's a wasp!" He let go of the rope with one of his hands and swatted madly at the air.

"Quentin!" his father yelled, dismayed.

Uh-oh, Pete thought. Never let go of the rope.

Instantly the boy's end of the piano dropped a foot and the other two men struggled against the shifting weight. The upright swung wildly to the left and then back to the right. Up in the window, Charlie was dragged half outside as the block and tackle twisted. "I can't hold it," he shouted.

Pete's stomach dropped as he saw the piano tilt further to the right. Quentin had now let go entirely and was stepping back rapidly. The upright slipped straight out of its sling and plummeted to the sidewalk. Quentin's father grabbed the other man and pulled him out of the way, just in time. Pete saw that if he'd stayed where he was, he would have been crushed.

The noise the piano made as it hit the concrete and shattered was like nothing Pete had ever heard before – wood screamed as it cracked and splintered and hundreds of metal strings twanged and broke. The cacophony went on and on and what had once been an upright piano was now a pile of black shards.

"Quentin! How could you have done that?" the father said as quietly as he could manage. "It was just a wasp."

"But I'm scared of wasps! You know that!" the son replied, almost crying.

"You're scared of a lot of things," his father said, very tightly.

By this time, someone had called the police, and soon a siren was wailing its way toward the scene. But the traffic started moving, and as the crowd thinned out in front of them, Pete and Bob were able to move again too.

"Wow," said Bob as they skirted the scene of the accident. "I kind of pity that kid."

"Me, too," said Pete. "I can't imagine dropping a rope like that, but he seems to have been thrown in at the deep end. Anyway, we've got to get going if we want to make it to the Salvage Yard on time. We don't want to be late for whatever Charlotte told Mallory she was going to tell us!"

"That's right," said Bob. "What do you think it is?"

"I don't know," Pete said. "Not really."

Still, secretly, he thought he *did* know. Two summers ago he'd gotten the idea that Charlotte Mitchell would like the Three Investigators' friend Connor O'Malley and that he'd like her back. And Pete had been right! Last summer Charlotte had moved up to Connor's place in Auburn. And as the old schoolyard chant went, First comes love, then comes .... But by now they'd arrived at the storefront window of Uncommon Treasures.

As always, the window was filled with an eclectic array of stuff – a map of Middle Earth, a tall earthenware jug, a hand-thrown tea set, a brown leather bomber jacket, a wooden flute. Stained glass suncatchers hung twirling from a steel rod.

Behind them, the police siren finally shut off.

"Let's go," Pete said. He opened the door and led the way inside. The shop was air-conditioned, and as the door silently closed behind them, the noise dimmed.

A middle-aged woman looked up at them, smiling. She was arranging brightly colored tee-shirts in a stack of wooden boxes. She had piercing eyes and salt-and-pepper hair and was wearing a caftan.

"Hello, Pete," she said. "What's all the ruckus?"

"Oh, hi, Mrs. Cantrell," Pete said. "Someone dropped a piano." He found he didn't want to go into it. "This is my friend Bob and we're here to buy a present for his father."

"Well, see what you like," the woman said. "If I can help, just give me a shout. Oh, wait! Look at this new display, Pete! It's your aunt and uncle's line of salves!"

Pete followed the line of her pointing finger and saw a colorful display of lip balms and hand creams and similar products – all of which had the words Robertsons' Remedies in fancy script across their lids.

"Wow!" he said to Bob. "Look at this! My aunt and uncle make these."

"You have an aunt and uncle with the last name of Robertson?" Bob asked as the two of them walked over to take a closer look.

"Sure. You know that," Pete said. "My mom's sister Lilliana and her husband Dave Robertson. And my three cousins, Mateo, Gabriella, and Estevan. Lilliana married an Anglo. My uncle inherited a small citrus grove in the San Joaquin Valley, near Bakersfield. The Golden Globe Citrus Grove. It's pretty little – only sixty acres –  so over the last few years they've been branching out into stuff like this. All organic and natural. My mom swears by them. She mentioned that Mrs. Cantrell was carrying them."

"Your mom's the one who turned me on to the whole line. My customers love them," Mrs. Cantrell interjected. "Well, I'll leave you to it." She walked off to talk with someone else, and Pete and Bob started browsing a long table by the door.

Pete knew that Bob wanted to find his father something he might be able to use for his writing, so he wasn't surprised when Bob picked up a fancy leather-bound journal, and then a silver pen, but his own eye was drawn to a cylindrical light orange box with the words WRITER'S DICE in brilliant green on the top.

He read the description, then took off the top of the box and poured some colorful dice onto the table.

"Have you ever heard of writing dice?" he asked Bob. "Look at this. It's some sort of a game. It says it can be used by either one or two people. Maybe you and your dad could play it together."

He and Bob studied the dice and discovered that there were twelve of them. Four of them were yellow and were marked Protagonist, Conflict, Setting, and Theme, and eight of them were marked with other words or phrases – some of them pretty bizarre.

"I guess you roll them and then have to make up a story with what you get," Pete said. "Like 'two-headed alien' and 'beauty queen' and 'desert island' and 'tarantula.'"

Bob laughed. "That would be quite a

story," he said.

"I bet you and your dad could have a lot of fun together with these," Pete said.

"I bet you're right," Bob said. "This is pretty perfect."

And it had hardly taken any time at all to find it!

"Did you discover something you like?" Mrs. Cantrell said when they went to the cash register. "Oh, Writer's Dice! I can't seem to keep that in stock!" She rang up the purchase and put it in a bag. "Be sure to say hello to your mother for me, Pete."

"I will, Mrs. Cantrell," Pete said. "She'll be happy you're carrying Aunt Lilli's balms! Thanks a lot."

Out on the street, Bob suddenly said, "Oh, no, I should have asked her to wrap it! Maybe she still can."

Pete glanced at his watch. "We've got forty minutes left before Wally and Isabella are due at the Salvage Yard," he said. "Let's grab our bikes and head to my house. My mom has tons of really cool wrapping paper."

As they turned off Main onto Sycamore Street, Pete could see that traffic was flowing, the ANDERSON MOVING truck was gone, and city workers with a front-loader and a dump truck were scooping up what was left of the piano.

It was only a five-minute bike ride to Pete's house, and when they got there, he was surprised to find both of his parents home. Only his mother had been there when he'd left. His father waved from the yard, where he was unloading some lumber from his pickup, and his mother greeted Bob with a hug, then went to find some silver paper to wrap Malcolm Andrews's present.

She was in her usual good mood, but when Pete mentioned the display of Robertsons' Remedies in Uncommon Treasures, she frowned. "It's funny you should mention Lilli," she said. "I'm actually pretty worried about her business. She and her husband are getting hassled by government bureaucrats. It was bad enough when the guy next door put in an amusement park – "

"What?" Pete said. "I don't remember you telling me about an amusement park."

His mother looked at him skeptically. "I'm sure I told you. You remember how a lot of families used to go to the grove to pick their own fruit? Well, after some rich guy bought the orchard next door, he used ten uncultivated acres of his land to put in a small amusement park. There's a merry-go-round, and a Ferris wheel, and a roller coaster, and I don't know what-all. Then he *also* started his own pick-your-own operation, and so, of course, all the families started going there, because the kids wanted the rides. He lets the children into the amusement park for a very small admission fee while the parents go to pick their fruit."

"That's a lot of trouble to get people to go to your orchard," Bob said.

"Lilli said he has money to burn," Valeria said. "It sure has caused problems for her and her husband. They still have a roadside stand for drop-by customers, and they still have the mail order business. Some people even have standing orders for every month. But they had to find another way to make money. Do you remember the goats?" she asked Pete.

"Sure!" Pete said. "Aunt Lilli had four, didn't she?"

Just then, Pete's father came in from the yard, and after washing his hands and drying them on a kitchen towel, he joined the conversation.

"Five," his mother said, "and she milked them every day. That was what gave her the idea for the balms and salves, actually − having all that extra milk. Goats' milk makes the best soap, and Robertsons' Remedies was a god-send. Without it they'd have gone under. But now they've branched out into supplements. And it seems the government is harassing them about it."

"The government, eh?" Pete's father said. "We're having trouble with them, too, on the set of the movie I'm working on this summer. There's a brand new agency called the California Rapid Response Health and Safety Commission."

"I think that's the name of the agency that's meddling with Robertsons' Remedies, too!" Pete's mother said. "You'd think they'd leave small companies and hard-working people alone!"

"They won't, though," Pete's father said. "There's enough red tape to tie up a herd of elephants. It seems that every county in the state now has two separate agencies – one for health and one for safety. The new system was supposed to simplify things, but all they've done is hire more bureaucrats who now have more time to stick their oars in everyone's business."

Pete's mother nodded agreement. "And if Lilli and David weren't having enough trouble, over the winter about twenty-five of their orange trees died," she said, shaking her head.

"Right in the middle of the orchard. We all hope there's a simple explanation. It's just weird that it's those trees and no others. They're having the soil tested to see why. They're supposed to get the results today."

She stopped and looked at Pete and Bob consideringly.

Uh-oh, Pete thought. He knew that look. It meant she'd had what she thought was a great idea, involving him. Though in this case, it seemed to involve not only him, but also Bob.

"So," his mother said, apparently changing the subject, "It's great that The Three Investigators are going to get a reward for finding that Fang Ngil mask. That should take away all of Jupiter's money worries for a while!"

"It already has," said Bob. "We're all really relieved."

"It's nice to have no money worries," Pete's mother said, nodding judiciously. "Of course, The Three Investigators have never really worked for money – just for the satisfaction of solving a case. And you know what I'm thinking, suddenly? I'm thinking that if you don't have a case at the moment, the two of you and Mallory and Jupiter might want to take a trip to Bakersfield to see if you can help

Lilli and her husband. Bakersfield isn't that far. Of course, when you're busy, two hours can seem like a lot. But if you're *not* busy – not exactly – ”

“I don't know, Mom,” said Pete. “Dead trees isn't exactly a *mystery*.”

“It's less than two hours,” his mother said, “and if you wanted to stay up there for a day or two, I'm sure it would be fine if you all stayed in the old goat shed.”

“Are the goats still there?” Pete asked. He remembered that they'd butted quite a lot.

“No,” his mother said. “They sold the goats. They get their goats' milk from a local creamery now. It would be pretty rustic, but you guys have never minded that, have you?”

“No,” Pete admitted. “But an old goat shed –” He was afraid that wouldn't sound all that appealing to Jupiter and Mallory  – or even to Bob, who had started smiling. To try to help Pete out, Bob asked, “How did Mr. Robertson come to inherit the Golden Globe to begin with?”

“Now, *that's* a story,” Pete's father said. “I always liked Dave's father, Charlie Robertson. What a character! He's been dead for more than twenty years now. He could talk a blue streak and he told the most amazing stories about the war."

"Which war?" Bob asked with genuine interest.

"World War Two," Pete's father said. "He went off to fight when he was just eighteen. Imagine that. Just a few years older than you. He was still alive when your mother and I got engaged. So we got to know him a little bit."

"He was a great guy," Pete's mother said, nodding vigorously.

"He was the son of a couple who came to California in the late 1920s," his father continued. "They'd been homesteaders in the Oklahoma Territory. But when the bottom fell out of the wheat market, Charlie's father lost the farm and decided to leave the state. This was before the Great Depression."

"Uncle David's father didn't have it easy," his mother said. "They were dirt poor when they got to the San Joaquin Valley. They took jobs as migrant laborers, picking fruit and other produce. Everyone looked down on them. Called them Okies. Or Arkies, if they were from Arkansas. They lived in tent camps and shanties they built themselves from scrap lumber. On the outskirts of the towns. They didn't have clean water or toilet facilities or anything really."

"It sounds like that movie we saw in eighth-grade History class," Pete said.

"*The Grapes of Wrath,*" said Bob.

"So how did Mr. Robertson get to own an orange orchard?" Pete asked.

"At some point, Charlie's parents moved away from the migrant camps to a small town called Lindsay, where they were able to buy a little shack to live in And, as I said, Charlie went off to fight in the Second World War as a foot soldier. Somehow he made it through un-scathed and came back to this country and went to college on the G.I. Bill," Pete's father said.

"I guess it was in his blood, so he studied agriculture. He eventually managed to buy that sixty-acre citrus grove. He wanted to buy more land and increase his operation, but it never happened. But he did plant lemons and tanger-ines and grapefruit as well as the oranges that were already there. He loved the work," his fa-ther went on. "And I'll always remember one afternoon not long before your mother and I got married. He took us for a walk through the orchard – Lilliana and David and me and your mother – "

"And he just climbed one of the orange

trees," his mother said, laughing. "Just like that, at his age. I don't know how he did it, but all of a sudden he was up in the branches, picking oranges and tossing them down to us. The sweetest oranges in the world."

"Everything he got came about through his own hard work," Pete's father said. "He made a really good life for himself and his family. It would be terrible if anything happened to the Golden Globe Citrus Grove."

Just then, the landline in the kitchen rang, and Pete's mother picked it up. "Oh, Lilli!" she said. "Martín, and I were just talking about you and Dave! Did you get the results of the test back yet?"

There was silence on Valeria's end of the phone call for a while, but soon she started murmuring, "Oh no! But why? Who would do that? It seems completely senseless!"

When she hung up, she turned to Pete and Bob with the same look in her eyes she'd had before – but now with a gleam of something like triumph.

"Well, here's a mystery for The Three Investigators," she said. "My sister got back the lab results on the soil around the dead orange trees. It wasn't a disease. Someone deliberately killed them. Someone poisoned them by putting salt around their roots!"

"Salt?" Bob said.

"That's terrible," Pete said.

"It's an ancient method of vanquishing your enemies," Pete's father said. "On a movie I worked on once, a conquering army in Biblical times destroyed an ancient city, then salted the fields around it to keep the people from rebuilding."

"Well, Lilli didn't tell me *that*," said Pete's mother, "but she *did* say that salt keeps plants from absorbing moisture – which of course kills them. And once salt gets into the soil, it's very hard to get out. It can last for decades."

Fixing Pete with a gimlet stare, she added, "Oh, Pete, you and the others *have* to try to help them now. To figure out who did this."

But although Pete was normally very impulsive when it came to helping people, in this case he was reluctant to commit The Three Investigators to an actual new case before he had the chance to talk with all of them about it. Luckily, Bob wasn't.

"I agree," said Bob. "We have to at least try. And I'm sure that once Jupiter and Mallory get the details about what's going on, they'll be as eager as I am to try to help your sister, Mrs. Crenshaw!"

Well, that was that, Pete thought. It looked as if The Three Investigators had a new case. And while Pete might personally have preferred to wait a little longer before he and Jupiter and Mallory and  Bob settled on where they headed next, it looked as if Bob had already started playing Writer's Dice, and the setting of his story was going to be Bakersfield, the protagonists were going to be Pete's aunt and uncle, the conflict was going to be the little guys against the big guys, and the theme – well, Pete had no idea what *that* would be until he saw how the case unfolded!

# 2

## **An Amazing Coincidence**

**B**ob, too, had been thinking about the game he'd bought at Uncommon Treasures, and as he pulled into the Salvage Yard on his bike twenty minutes later, he was glad he'd decided to stop by his own house first, to drop off the present for his father.

Since neither of Bob's parents was home, it had been a perfect time to smuggle it into his bedroom – although he almost wished Pete's mother hadn't wrapped it.

Not that she hadn't done a great job with the wrapping, but Writer's Dice had looked like a lot of fun – and since it could be played by either one person or two, Bob would have liked to try it out a bit before he gave it to his father. As he wheeled his bike to a stop and hit the kickstand, he was also thinking that it was strange that just last week his father had been threatened with the loss of his job, and this week Pete's aunt and uncle were being threatened with the loss of their business.

Of course, they were very different situations, but they shared a common denominator

– that the world could be a dangerous and un-predictable place to try to make a living. Pete's mother had been right when she said that The Three Investigators had been lucky to have no money worries at the moment.

The whole discussion with Pete's parents had been very interesting, actually. Bob couldn't remember ever before having heard them talk so much together about a single subject, and Mr. Crenshaw had really gotten into describing Charles Robertson's background – which wasn't all that different from the background of the migrant workers in *The Grapes of Wrath.*

That movie had made a big impression on Bob. He had always been interested in history, but he'd never before encountered that particular piece of American history. And while he would never have mentioned this to Pete, it was during the class in which they'd seen that film that Bob had first really thought about Pete's father's parents – poor farmers from Mexico who had come to California to make a new life, and how they'd worked as migrant laborers before they'd found jobs as gardeners in Los Angeles.

Really, Pete and his cousins were only two generations away from the kind of life his father and mother had just been describing. The thing was, when Bob had been at Pete's house listening to Mrs. Crenshaw, he'd felt The Three Investigators had no choice but to try to help the Robertsons. But now that he had gotten a little distance on the situation, he was thinking that maybe he should have looked before he leaped.

After all, although they might be able to find some leads on who had poisoned the Robertsons' trees, there was nothing they could do about the fact that some rich dude had bought the land next door to them and siphoned off their you-pick-it business. As for the government agency that had started to harass them about Robertsons' Remedies, well, there was *less* than nothing  they could do about *that*!

Bob's father was fond of reminding anyone in the range of his voice that the 40th President of the United States had once said that the most terrifying words in the English language were "I'm from the Government and I'm here to help!" His point had been that anything a government agency got involved with was almost bound to make the situation worse – although once it *was* involved, there was no way on earth to make it go away.

If that was true – and Bob knew from

his general life experience that it *must* be − then he and Pete should have simply told Mrs. Crenshaw that The Three Investigators couldn't possibly help her sister − not if the government was involved.

Well, Bob thought, as he started walking toward HQ2, maybe it wasn't too late to call the whole thing off − to find some other case. for their second case of the summer. Before he'd left the Crenshaw's house, Bob had told Pete that if he wanted, he should wait until Bob arrived at the Salvage Yard to tell Mallory and Jupiter what had happened − though he had the uneasy feeling that Pete probably hadn't done that.

After all, Wally Tate, Isabella Chang, and Charlotte Mitchell were due any time now, and Pete would have wanted to bring Jupe and Mallory up to speed before they arrived. As he walked into HQ2, Bob saw that Jupiter, Mallory, and Pete were all sitting in beanbag chairs in the part of their new Headquarters that had been set aside for informal lounging.

Their old Headquarters − a now-rusty and always-dented old mobile home trailer that Jupiter's uncle had let him use − had grown too small for them as they'd gotten older. Though Bob knew he'd always love HQ1, it was cramped and a bit gloomy in comparison to HQ2, an old shed in the Jones Salvage Yard that they'd recently finished renovating in accordance with Mallory's plans.

HQ2 was spacious and light-filled and cheerful. Aside from the hang-out area, there was a more formal arrangement with a sofa and chairs where they could meet new clients and entertain guests, an office where they could work and do research, and a kitchen where they could make themselves a snack, all gathered together in one big open space.

HQ2 was quite a change from HQ1 – which had been the boys' secret, and which Jupiter had allowed almost no one to ever see. So far several people connected to their first case of the summer had been inside HQ2, and they'd shown the place to Jupiter's aunt and uncle and to their old friend Worthington. But Isabella and Wally would be the first of their favorite clients to tour the place.

Bob hung his backpack on a hook, threw himself into the other beanbag chair, and took a deep breath. But before he could even start his explanation of all the reasons why  he had changed his mind about The Three Investigators trying to help Pete's aunt and uncle, Pete flashed him a broad grin.

"They said yes!" he crowed. "Though we're just going to go up to Bakersfield for the day, to start with. I didn't think Jupiter and Mallory would be thrilled by the idea of sleeping in a goat shed, and I was right! Still, if we start off early, we can get there before lunch, and I've already called Worthington and he says he can take us up tomorrow – though he won't be able to start 'til 10:00."

Bob could hardly remember the last time he had been so unhappy to see someone grin. It was clearly too late now to say that he'd changed his mind. Instead, he said, "Well, if you really think we can do something. So, Jupe, have you got any good ideas about how to find out who salted the trees?"

"Not yet," said Jupiter. "But Pete's father was right. Salting trees seems a savage and vindictive act. Roman generals salted the fields of the people they conquered. Still, it's too early to speculate as to what is really going on – though the presence of a rich neighbor does suggest certain time-honored possibilities. However, since our visitors are due any time now, I think we should wait until after they've come and gone to continue the discussion."

With that, at least, Bob agreed. The Three Investigators had met Isabella Chang and Wally Tate two summers before, on two different cases. Pete had thought they might really like each other, and sure enough, they were now sharing Isabella's house. They were both retired high school teachers. Isabella was in her 80s and Wally was now 96.

As for Charlotte Mitchell, she'd been working for Isabella when they'd met her. She was now living up north in Auburn with their artist friend Connor O'Malley. Pete had also matched *them* up. Charlotte was down in Rocky Beach for a short visit, and she was driving Wally and Isabella over to the Salvage Yard so that they could see HQ2.

Just then Bob heard the familiar crunch of gravel that meant a car had driven into the yard.

"That must be Charlotte," Jupiter said, jumping to his feet. Bob and the others followed him out to see that Charlotte had parked in the shade near the office, and she stood waving as Wally helped Isabella out of the back seat. "Yoo hoo, you guys," Charlotte called. "Connor sends greetings."

Wally was dressed in a plaid button-down shirt and khaki trousers. He wore a round cotton hat with a brim to keep the sun off his almost bald head. Bob remembered him saying that baldness ran in his family – that his father had been so forgetful he'd lost his hair in his thirties and had never been able to find it again!

"Isabella," Mallory said. "You look really nice."

Isabella was wearing a summery dress and a pair of hip-looking sunglasses. She had trouble with her eyes and was, in fact, legally blind.

"Thank you, my dear," she said. "I always dress up for a party."

"Wally!" Pete said. "Good to see you!"

Wally, who was never at a loss for words, stood staring at the front of HQ2. "My, oh my," he said. "What a beautiful job you've done. I love the dormers. And the cupola."

"Mallory designed it all," Pete said.

"With lots of help," Mallory said.

The seven of them went back inside and Charlotte, Isabella, and Wally exclaimed in surprise and pleasure as Mallory took them from one area to another. They wound up at the back wall, with its high clerestory windows, on which The Three Investigators were displaying the mementos they'd collected from all their recent cases.

"Tell us about each one," Isabella said.

"Don't leave anything out."

Isabella seemed delighted to see the antique assayer's scale Gordon Small had given them as a memento of the case that had involved her. And Wally was pleased to see the carved whale that Rafael Solares had given them for the case that had involved animal smuggling in which Wally's own son had been involved.

"Look!" Charlotte said. "There's the dagger that Madhuri Singh had! And the kaleidoscope from Odetta Dharmapuki." Those were the two cases that Charlotte had been most intimately connected to – one at the Rocky Beach Summer Theatre Festival and the other up in Auburn in a strange case that had involved kidnapping, gaslighting, fire bombs, and witches.

"This is quite remarkable," Wally said. "It's not just a new Headquarters. It's like a Three Investigators museum. Perhaps you could hire me and Isabella as docents to give the curious public guided tours. We'd only keep a small percentage of the entrance fee."

"We'll let you know when crowds start clamoring for admittance," Bob said.

"You do that," Wally said, patting him on the shoulder. "But don't wait too long. Isabella and I may take another job."

"Oh, Wally," Isabella said, laughing. "You know you're my full-time job."

Wally grinned. "Mathematics was never my specialty, but congratulations times two on this marvelous building. As my old pappy used to say, You done good."

Bob took Isabella's arm and escorted her to one of the easy chairs in the more formal seating area. When all of them were comfortably arranged, Wally and Isabella looked at Charlotte expectantly.

"Are you going to tell them your big news?" Wally asked. He turned to Bob and the others. "As it turns out," he said confidentially, "you're not the only ones to be congratulated."

Pete grinned and clapped his hands together. "I knew it!" he said.

Charlotte looked very happy, but also embarrassed. "As it turns out, I'm going to be moving full-time up to Auburn. Because Connor and I are going to get married. Pete, you're a miracle worker. How did you know?"

"He just has a sixth sense about these things," Mallory said. "And he has a tendency to be right."

"I know!" Charlotte said. "He ought to hang out a shingle. He fixed up Wally and Isabella. And now my aunt Phillipa is in Wyoming for the summer. With Hector Sebastian."

That *had* been another of Pete's successes, Bob thought.

"Anyway," Charlotte said, "the wedding's going to be in Ojai, where I grew up. I want you all to be there."

"When is it?" Mallory asked.

"It's three weeks from Saturday," Charlotte said. "At the Tahiti Ojai Resort. We're having a treasure hunt and there'll be swimming, and a buffet lunch and a sit-down dinner. And dancing afterwards."

"Very fancy!" Pete said. Bob could see that Pete was really excited.

"You should all bring someone, too, if you want," Charlotte said.

"So I can bring Califia?" Pete asked.

"Absolutely," Charlotte said. "I was hoping you'd bring her. If not, I was going to invite her myself. After all, we bonded at the Wiccan circle up in Auburn."

She turned to Jupiter and Mallory with a questioning look. Jupiter shook his head no.

"Maybe Worthington!" Mallory said laughing. "He'll be driving us anyway. At least I hope so!"

"And Bob?" Charlotte said. "What

about you?"

Bob blushed, not as badly as Pete would have, but bad enough. "Probably not," he said. "But maybe."

Maybe, he thought, he ought to ask Freya Haldorsson. Still, he didn't want to commit to anything by saying her name out loud. He looked at Pete, who had recently encouraged him to go for it, and who seemed ready to say something when Bob shook his head faintly. Luckily, Pete got the message.

"Now," Wally said. "Enough yee-hawing. Are you four involved in a new case? That one with the African mask was really something."

He looked from Jupiter to Mallory to Pete to Bob, and when no one else said anything, Bob spoke up. "Maybe," he said. "Pete's aunt is having some troubles with her citrus business up near Bakersfield and we're going to be looking into it."

"A citrus business?" Wally asked.

"She and my uncle own an orange grove," Pete said. "And they also grow lemons and limes and things. My aunt married a man named David Robertson who inherited the place from his father Charles."

Wally did a double take. "Did you say

Charles? Charles Robertson?"

"I'm pretty sure that was his name," Pete said.

"Do you remember the name of the business?" Wally asked.

"It's called the Golden Globe Citrus Grove," Pete said.

"Well, butter my bald head and call me a biscuit!" Wally exclaimed, slapping his knee. "Charlie Robertson was a really good friend of mine. What are the odds that his only son would marry your mother's sister?"

"You know my aunt?" Pete asked, astounded.

"I wouldn't say I *know* her," Wally said. "But I met her and David while Charlie was still alive, though I have to admit I'd never have remembered their names. I haven't seen them since the funeral. It was too hard to stay in touch."

"Why?" Pete asked.

"Charlie Robertson was my best friend when I was growing up," Wally said. "His death was quite a shock to me. He'd just turned 70 when he died. He got his Biblical three score and ten, but I thought he had a lot more tread on his tires. These days we old codgers expect to live a lot longer than 70 before we enter the Great Beyond. Why, look at Isabella and me!"

"How did you meet him?" Bob asked.

"We were both Okies," Wally said, "so we were sort of thrown together. His parents were Elmer and Gertrude Robertson and they moved themselves and Charlie to the San Joaquin Valley when things didn't work out back in Oklahoma.

"They got to California sooner than my parents did, in the late 20s, I think, so Charlie was born here. I was born back in Oklahoma and was even more of an Okie than he was – though we both had Okie accents. We never really lost our accents, not completely, but we both had the dubious privilege of fighting in the war and then going to college on the G.I. Bill.

"I became a high school teacher and Charlie went and bought himself an orange grove. Charlie was a little older than I was, but we shared just about everything in our childhoods, including working for the Central California Ice Company. Its headquarters was in Lindsay, where we grew up, at a place called the Ice House, on Sweet Briar Avenue."

"You made ice cubes?" Pete asked.

Wally laughed. "Those were the days before electric refrigerators, Pete. Charlie and I

40

cut blocks of ice with ice picks and delivered them to peoples' houses. People had what were called ice boxes – wooden boxes lined with zinc for the most part. The ice went into a space in the bottom and kept the rest of the ice box cool.

"It was great to work in the Ice House on those hot summer days. It was so cold we had to wear jackets! It was very hard physical work, but we both liked doing something real that helped other people. It was terrific to be so young and to be making real money. You should have seen our muscles! Neither one of us – Charlie in particular – liked team sports, but if we'd been boxers, I bet we could have licked just about anyone we went to school with, we were that strong."

"Boy," Pete said. "I can just see you as a boxer. Pow, pow!" He punched the air with his fists.

"Happily, we both made it through the war," Wally said. "As you know, I got shot and ended up with a bit of a bum leg. But Charlie got by without a scratch. It was a microscopic fungus that did him in. When he was in his mid-forties, he got very sick. He came down with a high fever and a cough, and he was tired all the time. Valley fever. There's a fungus

41

in the soil of the San Joaquin Valley – it's in lots of places, really – and when the soil gets churned up, the fungus enters the air and people breathe it in and it makes them sick."

"It's also called California fever," said Isabella, "and sometimes desert rheumatism."

"Anyway," Wally went on, "Charlie got very sick with it, and there was nothing you could do for it in those days. He was in bed for weeks and was never the same afterwards. He always thought his lungs had been permanently damaged. Valley Fever wasn't on the death certificate, but you can bet that it was partly responsible for the fact that he only lived to be 70."

"Is there a cure for Valley Fever now?" Bob asked.

"Not that I know of," said Wally. "Though I bet some company somewhere is trying to find one! But what's the problem you're going to be looking into up in Bakersfield?"

Together, Pete and Bob explained – though Bob feared it wasn't the best explanation he'd ever given. Even worse, the more he tried to explain the problem, the more unlikely it seemed that The Three Investigators could ever solve it. He didn't usually feel that way at the beginning of a case, but as he tried to describe this one, it all seemed amazingly nebulous. So nebulous that he suddenly found himself saying just that.

"What does nebulous mean again?" asked Pete.

It was Wally who answered Pete's question. "It means lacking definition – indistinct, unformed, amorphous. But I actually don't agree with Bob that it's indistinct – it's sprawling. There seem to be three problems, not just one. The poisoning of the orange trees with salt, the amusement park set up by the rich guy, and the government agency harassing The Golden Globe Citrus Grove. Those government agencies are the worst. What's this new one called again?"

"The California Rapid Response Health And Safety Commission," Bob said.

"Well, well," said Wally. "I guess even if you can't provide a cure for Valley Fever, you can always be an orange-grove botherer." He looked at Pete shrewdly. "If you're really planning to go to Bakersville, maybe you'd consider taking me with you. I've been to your aunt and uncle's place before. What did you say their names were again?"

"Lilliana and David," Pete said.

"Lilliana and David," Wally said. "Yes, I met them several times. It would give me a lot of pleasure to see Charlie's son after all these years, and to see the orange groves again. How will you be getting up there?"

"Worthington will be driving us," Bob explained. "We're old enough to get our learner's permits, and we'll get them any time now. But we made a pact not to learn to drive until after the summer is over so that we can spend our time solving new cases."

"A wise decision," Wally said. "Besides, who wants to put themselves at the mercy of the DMV? The best thing about your not driving is that you haven't had to deal with that idiotic bunch of nincompoops."

"The DMV?" Mallory asked.

"The Division of Motor Vehicles," Wally said, "one of the most rigid bureaucracies in the world. I've often wondered if you have to submit to having your humanity sucked out of you by a great big tube to get a job with it. Whatever Pete's aunt and uncle have gotten twisted up with, it can't possibly be worse than the California DMV."

"You sound as if you speak from experience," said Jupiter.

"You bet," said Wally. "I'd been in the

Army, mind you, and I'd dealt with high school administrators. But nothing like this." He sat quietly and folded his arms on his chest.

"So what happened?" Mallory asked.

Wally snorted. "I get angry all over again just thinking about it. It was fifteen years ago now, I reckon. I was eighty-one the last time I went in to renew my license. By that time I'd had a California driver's license for over sixty years, and for most of that time at the same address.

"I filled out the paperwork and pushed it across the counter at a young woman who couldn't have been older than thirty. She should have been a prison guard. Who knew such hard-eyed stony-faced people existed? She typed into a computer and then looked back at me with those cold blue eyes and just shook her head."

"She wouldn't let you renew your license?" Mallory asked. "Why not?"

"She told me the State of Nevada had put a hold on the renewal," said Wally. "It seemed that forty years earlier, when I was in my forties, I'd gotten a speeding ticket in Nevada. It was during a year I was teaching at a small college in southern Utah, and I'd never paid the ticket. In those days they didn't hand it to you the way they do now; they mailed it to you.

"When computers came along, someone with nothing better to do had gone through all the old files and entered old unpaid parking and speeding and traffic tickets into a big computer database. Now, California wanted me to pay a forty-year-old speeding ticket I'd gotten in another state. With interest!

"Well, I did it, a week or two later," Wally continued, "but I was so aggravated that I went to the trouble of asking to see all the paperwork from Nevada. I had no memory of the ticket in the first place. So here's the punch line: The cop who pulled me over had terrible handwriting, and when he wrote down the address in Utah where I was staying so they could send me my ticket, his "U" in the postal code for Utah looked like a V. So they sent my ticket to an address in Vermont. Of course I never got it − and forty years later it came back to bite me. To me, that's government bureaucracy in a nutshell. A really nasty nutshell."

"Wow!" Pete said. "That really *is* a horrible story."

"What makes it even worse," Wally said, "is that all the bureaucrats think they're members of one big family, so they stick together. I got absolutely no sympathy – not in Nevada, and not in California – even though it was Nevada's fault that the paperwork had gotten fouled up to begin with. That woman at the California DMV was ready to support some faceless person she'd never met rather than be sympathetic to me, when I was standing right in front of her. Bureaucracies attract the worst kind of people – or turn people into them. Who knows what they'd do with their lives if they couldn't be bureaucrats? Maybe become vicious killers."

Jupiter, Mallory, and Pete all laughed at this, and even Isabella smiled, but Bob felt very gloomy. He couldn't remember a previous time when Wally had been this sardonic, and both Wally's attitude and his story made Bob feel even more foolish for having told Mrs. Crenshaw that The Three Investigators should be able to help her sister.

While there was some slight chance they might be able to figure out who had poisoned the orange trees, there was clearly no chance they'd be able to help with anything else.

Although *any* failure on the part of The Three Investigators would be disappointing, for them to fail in a case that involved one of their families would be more than disappointing; it would be a true disaster – and when the word "disaster" entered Bob's mind unbidden, so did an alarming vision of a teenage boy named Quentin dropping the rope he was holding, and a black piano crashing in ruins on the sidewalk.

3

## Closed By Health And Safety!

The following morning, Mallory got to the Salvage Yard early, so that she could do a little work for Aunt Mathilda before Worthington arrived at 10:00 to whisk her and the others off to Bakersfield. Now she was sitting in a shed with her laptop, typing a description of a mischievous plaster cherub that Uncle Titus had bought from a deconsecrated church.

She normally loved these early mornings at the Salvage Yard, but today she was feeling a little worried about Bob. Well, not worried exactly. Slightly concerned. The day before, after Charlotte had driven Wally and Isabella away, The Three Investigators had also all taken off, and she'd found herself bicycling next to Bob. He'd told her that he wished they'd never even *thought* of taking this case — though for heaven's sake not to tell Pete or Jupiter how he felt.

Naturally, she'd told him that she wouldn't — but even after he'd explained why he thought it had been a bad idea to promise Pete's mother they'd try to help her sister when they really didn't know  if they could, Mallory hadn't quite understood Bob's feeling. She actually thought he might still be reacting to what had happened during their last case − in the course of which he and the others had seen the age-old strategy of divide-and-conquer in action. He had taken it very personally when he and Pete had found themselves being treated preferentially compared to Jupiter and Mallory.

Funnily enough, Mallory herself hadn't regretted the experience. In the great scheme of things, it had been pretty minor, as well as having been arranged for an obvious reason by a set of white-collar villains. And, anyway, the longer she'd lived in California, the more interested she'd become in how complex the history and culture of America was, and how bizarre it was that so many people seemed to want to force that complexity into tidy little boxes.

The messiness was what made life interesting − every person different from every other, a mix of genetics, experiences, cultures, races, histories. Sure, everybody was like some other people, but what made them interesting was not their similarities but their differences.

Through her work with The Three Investigators, Mallory had discovered that all you needed to do was travel two hours in just about any direction to discover a whole new subculture in California. There was the Serbian community in Jackson that centered on St. Sava's Serbian Orthodox Church, the Greek community in Santa Barbara, the wine-growing community in the Napa Valley, the small community of people who lived on houseboats in Sausalito, her friend Hiroka among them. And that wasn't even scratching the surface.

Maybe that was why road trip novels and movies were such a popular genre in the United States. A whole new world was just a car ride away. She was going to be very interested to see Bakersfield and the San Joaquin Valley – and not from the window of a speeding car. But now, as she finished the  description she'd been typing, she was jolted by the full-throated roar of a motorcycle's tailpipes. She jumped to her feet and looked out the door of the shed. The noise had also brought Aunt Mathilda and Uncle Titus out of the Salvage Yard's office and onto the porch.

The roar came to an abrupt halt. Mallory watched as a man got off the Harley Davidson and leaned it on its kickstand. He was nothing like anyone she would ever have seen in Scotland – or in Rocky Beach for that matter. Another amazing variation on an

American.

He took off his helmet and balanced it on the saddle. He wore dark wraparound sunglasses, like the eyes of a very large insect. He had a scraggly beard, but as far as she could see, he was totally bald – whether by heredity or choice she couldn't tell. A red bandana was knotted around his neck, and a small silver cross hung from his left ear by a thin silver chain. He was wearing leather pants, punched with silver studs, and a sleeveless tee-shirt. His biceps bulged.

The Salvage Yard seemed very quiet in the wake of the tailpipes' roar. Uncle Titus had descended the office steps and was approaching the man – who took off his sunglasses and stuck out his hand to shake Uncle Titus's. Mallory could see his eyes were mild and he had a disarming smile.

"Robert Ackers," the man said. "Though my friends call me Cueball."

"Pleased to meet you, Cueball," Uncle Titus said. "Though I don't think we're at the friendship stage yet, do you? I'm Titus Jones, the owner of this establishment. Can I help you?"

"Titus – ," Aunt Mathilda called from the office porch.

"You go on, Mathilda," Uncle Titus said. "I'll take care of this."

Aunt Mathilda nodded and went back inside.

Robert Ackers – Cueball – looked around. He was calm and unhurried and he had a friendly air about him as though he were open to experiences of every kind.

"I may be wrong," he said. "But my eyes tell me this isn't the kind of salvage yard I was expecting. I thought you might have some spare bike parts."

Uncle Titus looked slightly offended – though possibly also slightly worried. "Young man," he said – Mallory judged that Cueball was in his mid-to-late thirties – "this is the finest salvage yard west of the Mississippi. We have one of everything in the known universe. What do you need?"

Cueball smiled. "I'm looking for a throttle slide for my carburetor," he said.

"A throttle slide," Titus said as though there was a whole box of them in one of the sheds.

Cueball nodded. "Mine's sticking, and I thought I'd see if I could fix it."

Uncle Titus had glanced around and was surprised to see Mallory standing in the door of the shed where she was working. He beckoned to her. "Let me check with my assistant," he said.

Mallory headed over to where the two men were standing. Uncle Titus put a reassuring hand on her shoulder.

"This is Mallory MacLeod," he said to Cueball. "She knows every item in this whole dang place. Mallory, this is Mr. Ackers. He's looking for a throttle slide. For his carburetor."

Cueball smiled and offered his hand. "Hello, young lady," he said courteously.

His shake was warm and firm.

"I'm sorry, Mr. Ackers," Mallory began – stopping when she realized she didn't quite know how to put into words what she needed to say.

The man's eyes lit up. "Way cool accent," he said. "It's Scottish, right? Please call me Cueball," he said. "Everyone does."

Mallory was amazed he knew she was Scottish, but she went on with what she had steeled herself to say.

"I don't think we have any motorcycle parts anywhere in the Salvage Yard," she said.

Cueball smiled again, and this time also shrugged his shoulders.

"No problem," he said. "I was beginning

to get that idea. Well, I guess I'll have to take the bike to Skeet. He's my mechanic, expensive as all get-out. Me and my gang are headed up north and I want the slide fixed before then."

Mallory couldn't help herself. "You're part of a motorcycle gang?"

Cueball laughed. "Not at all," he said. "I meant my posse – my homeboys. Rooster and Knuckles and Buzz. We've been friends since forever."

"Where did you get names like that?" Mallory asked.

Cueball pointed to his head. "In my case, do you have to ask?"

"Just the four of you, eh?" Uncle Titus said. "And where up north are you headed? San Francisco?"

Cueball laughed again. "Man," he said. "We ain't city boys. I live near San Diego now, but I was born and raised in Bakersfield and that's as city as I ever want to get. Me and the gang are headed up there in a day or two – to stop in and see the family and some old friends."

"Wow!" Mallory said. "My friends and I are headed to Bakersfield, too." She suddenly wondered if they could be called a posse.

"If that's the case," Cueball said, "be

sure you stay at the Oasis. It's a down home motel – good people – and right across from the best country western bar in southern California. The Roundup. Barbecue, cold beer, and line dancing. A little bit of heaven."

"We're not actually staying there," Mallory said. "We're just going up for the day. And Bakersfield isn't really up north, is it?"

"We'd just be passing through," Cueball said. "My brother Denny has a business there. I see family, we stay at the Oasis, eat at the Roundup. Then we're headed to Idaho. There's a town called Elk Bend we go to every summer, way up in the Panhandle. And then we head off into the National Forest."

"With your bikes?" Mallory asked.

"We leave our bikes at the roadhead," Cueball said, "and hoof it."

"Camping!" Mallory said. Her mind was whirling. She'd thought of bikers as urban types who hung out at bars and rode in packs. At least that was what she'd gathered from pop culture.

"The great outdoors," Cueball said. "Where we can get away from all the people trying to tell us how to live our lives. We do that again, in a different way, every year in August, when we go to a biker's convention in

South Dakota. That's when all the bikers in the West hit the open road at once."

"The open road," Uncle Titus said enthusiastically. "That's what I love about my business, too. Whenever I'm feeling a bit – well, how should I put it?" He looked off in the direction of Aunt Mathilda – who never ran out of things for other people to do.

"I get in my truck and go looking for bargains," Uncle Titus said. "There's a freedom in being able to get up and go."

"That's the word," Cueball said. "Me and my friends are big on being able to make our own decisions without any meddling from dumb bureaucrats and lying politicians. If you'll pardon my language, Miss Mallory."

Mallory laughed. "I like it," she said, sincerely. "Too many people are scared to say what they really think these days."

"Isn't *that* true?" said Cueball. "Well," he added, stepping back toward his bike. "I won't take up any more of your valuable morning."

"Not at all, not at all," Uncle Titus said. "Are you sure I can't interest you in a –  . What did you find this morning, Mallory?"

"A fine example of a plaster cherub," Mallory said.

Cueball didn't miss a beat. "You

wouldn't happen to have a seraphim hanging around, would you?" he said slyly.

Mallory grinned.

"Not today," she said.

Cueball straddled the saddle of his bike and fastened on his helmet. Now he just looked like a motorcyclist instead of one of the most interesting people Mallory had met in a while.

"Maybe I'll run into you up in Bakersfield," he said. He put his hand to his visor in a small salute. "Thanks for your time, Mr. Jones," he said. "Enjoy the open road."

He revved his engine, swerved on a dime, and was gone through the Salvage Yard's gates – leaving Mallory suddenly wishing she and the others really *would* be staying in Bakersfield, at the Oasis Motel, across from the Roundup. She still had a lot to learn about American life, and the best way to do it really *had* to be from the inside of all its amazing subcultures.

Even though the San Joaquin Valley was actually quite close to Rocky Beach and the area around Los Angeles, Mallory had only seen it and the rest of the Central Valley through the windows of the Flex, on Interstate 5, when The Three Investigators had traveled north.

The evening before, however, she'd done some reading. The Central Valley ran between the coastal range to the west and the Sierra Nevadas to the east, a width of between 40 and 60 miles. It ran from Bakersfield in the south to Redding in the north, about 450 miles from south-southeast to north-northwest. It was rich flat agricultural land, watered by irrigation, and it harbored, next to Florida, the biggest citrus industry in the world.

But oranges and lemons and limes were not all that grew there. Central Valley farms grew table grapes and almonds, avocados and apricots, asparagus and tomatoes. Mallory had read that it produced half the fruits, vegetables, and nuts grown in the United States. There were also oil fields in the south, in Kern County where Bakersfield was.

Between the farms, orchards, and oil fields, it had a very different sort of population than Los Angeles did – much poorer in general, more working class. Hispanics made up almost half the population. Many people never finished high school and fewer still went on to college, Mallory had learned.

Now, she closed her laptop, signed her time sheet and closed the door to the shed behind her. Not long afterwards, Pete and Bob swung through the Salvage Yard's gates and, shortly afterwards, Worthington drove in and parked his car. When Jupiter also showed up, he and Worthington pulled up the Flex's third row seat and the five of them set off for Isabella Chang's to pick up Wally Tate.

That had been quite a story he had told the afternoon before, Mallory thought, as he emerged from the house and walked toward the car. Soon he was sitting next to Worthington in the front seat of the Flex, while Bob and Mallory sat behind him in the second row, and Pete and Jupiter sat on the bench seat. The spread-out nature of this seating arrangement made it next to impossible for the six of them to have a conversation, and soon Mallory found herself falling asleep.

When she woke an hour or more later, she looked out the window at the passing landscape. They were getting closer to Bakersfield, and though much of the land was flat, flat, flat, there were some dips and rises. It was very rural, miles and miles of fields without a house in sight. In the distance, to the east, she could see the hazy foothills of the Sierras.

They passed ordered ranks that could have been nut trees, Mallory thought, as well as fields of crops low in the fields – lettuce or beans. Heat shimmered as it rose from the ground. Then they started passing what Mallory suspected were orange groves.

"We're close to my aunt and uncle's place now," Pete said. He was sitting forward, grasping the back of Mallory and Bob's seat and staring out the window. "Look!" he said.

Mallory saw rows of orange trees, and in the distance the top of a Ferris wheel towering over the trees, and the twists and turns of a roller coaster. A brightly painted sign held aloft by two posts arched over a dirt drive that led into the grove. On one side of the sign was a merry-go-round and on the other was a bunch of oranges. Between them were the words The Citrus and Carnival Ranch.

"Is this the amusement park next to your aunt and uncle's?" Mallory asked.

"It must be," said Pete.

Worthington slowed down almost to a stop, and as they crept past, Wally looked at the sign with the merry-go-round and the oranges.

"Did you see that?" he asked, as they passed it.

"See what?" Bob asked.

"It said in small letters at the bottom of the sign 'Franklin Weaver, Proprietor,'" Wally said. "I knew a kid named Franklin Weaver when I was growing up in Lindsay. Really obnoxious. He was the son of a very rich man who owned the biggest and most successful general store in town. Maybe on the way back we can stop and see what all the fuss is about."

"Let's do it!" Pete said. "I haven't been here since the amusement park was built. I didn't even *know* about it until my mom told me the other day. But you know me. I *love* carnivals. And it's got a water slide!"

It wasn't far to the Golden Globe Citrus Grove, which had its own sign. "Welcome," Mallory read. "Drive on in! It's Valencia season! The best fruit in the Valley! Lemons! Limes! Robertsons' Remedies!"

Worthington turned right, down a straight-as-a-ruler dirt road. They passed rows and rows of orange trees. Oranges hung heavy on a lot of them. After a short drive, they entered a large clearing where a rambling old white farmhouse surrounded by shade trees stood. Behind it was a building with a metal roof, and to the side a wooden shed that Mallory supposed had once held the fabled goats.

There was also a stout square building with an open garage-type door. Over the door was a sign that read "Fruit Stand and Robertsons' Remedies." On either side were old half-barrels in which marigolds, petunias, and geraniums bloomed. Inside the stand, Mallory could see displays of oranges and other fruit, waiting to be bought. Off to the side was a small pond.

As Worthington came to a stop, a woman hurried out of the farmhouse door. She had short dark hair and a wide tan face. She wore a man's button-down shirt, whose tails she'd tied over her stomach, and a pair of shorts. She radiated warmth and authority.

"Aunt Lilli!" Pete cried as he ran to hug her. Everyone else piled out but Wally. Bob went over and helped him out of the car and then the two of them, together with Jupiter, Worthington, and Mallory, went over to be introduced to Pete's aunt. Pete gave his aunt presents from his mother – a dreamcatcher to snare any evil spirits that might be roaming at night and an aqua quartz crystal on a silver chain for good luck. She laughed as she slipped the chain round her neck.

"These are my friends, Aunt Lilli," Pete said. "Jupiter Jones and Bob Andrews are the other two members of The Three Investigators, and Mallory MacLeod is our Special Consultant. William Worthington is our friend and driver. And this is Wally Tate. Do you remember him?"

Aunt Lilli looked closely at Wally.

"I met you and your husband many years ago," Wally said, "when your husband's father Charles was still alive. He and I grew up together in Lindsay during the Depression."

"Wally Tate," Lilliana said, astonished. "Of course I remember you. I remember you and Charlie talking about the Ice House."

"It was a pleasure meeting you, Mrs. Robertson," Worthington said. He turned to Jupiter. "I'm going to take off now and see a bit of Bakersfield. I'll be back when you call me." He strode back to the Flex and was soon out of sight, down the driveway.

Just then the door of the farmhouse opened and a man and two teenagers came out. "Uncle David!" Pete said, running to shake his hand. David Robertson was tall and well-built. He was in his 50s and his hair had started to gray. The teenagers were Pete's cousins.

Estevan, almost as tall as his father, had a brash smile and a brush of black hair. Gabriella was more shy. She had long dark hair pulled back in a ponytail. They were both delighted to see Pete. He was kidding around with

Estevan about spending the night in the goat shed when Pete's uncle came over.

"What a pleasant surprise to see you again, Mr. Tate," he said.

Wally laughed. "Call me Wally," he said. "Please."

"My father used to talk about you all the time," David Robertson said. "He looked up to you. Said you were the brains of the operation, he was the brawn."

"Charlie was plenty smart," Wally said. "I miss him. It was wonderful to have him in my life as I got older. He shared my memories, both the good and the bad – the bad mostly being some of the other kids we went to school with."

"What a coincidence that you know Pete," David Robertson said. "Come. Let me show you our farm stand."

He led the way through the open garage-type door. Daylight flooded in through the windows on three sides. On the left, all the fruit was beautifully displayed – oranges, lemons, limes, apricots – and on the other side were display shelves for Robertsons' Remedies – tubes and pots and bottles of unguents, salves, and lotions, as well as dark glass bottles in serried rows. With the overriding smell of citrus fruit in the air, the place exuded well-being. What a nice place this was, really, Mallory thought.

She wandered over to look at the products the Robertsons made, picking up one after the other – soaps and hand creams and shampoos and hair rinses, shaving creams and herbal salves and lip balms. All of them were made with organic ingredients and a lot of them had citrus in them. The supplements included Sleep Support and Digestive Support and Immune Support. Off to the side was a stand-alone cardboard display holding little bottles of something called San Joaquin Valley Supplement.

As Mallory picked up a bottle and began to read the label, Pete's aunt said, "That's our latest success. Our older son Mateo dreamed it up. Since his grandfather almost died of Valley fever when he was in his forties, Mateo thought it would be a good idea to offer a supplement that specially pumped up the immune system against viruses and bacteria – and fungi like the one that causes Valley fever."

"Does it work?" Mallory asked.

"People swear by it," Pete's aunt said. "We've been selling it for over a year now and it's far and away our best seller. You wouldn't believe the number of testimonials we've gotten from satisfied customers. They're all collected in that little book."

She pointed. Mallory saw a small black notebook with a hole punched in the back cover, hanging from a stainless steel chain attached to the display.

"Of course, we never make claims for it that aren't true, but even so, it's a big hit."

"Our children have been an incredible help," Pete's uncle said. "Gabriella handles the fruit. She's going to be a senior in high school in the fall, but she managed to organize all our mail order customers."

Just then, a white sedan with a seal on the driver's door pulled into the clearing, and a man got out. He was wearing a khaki uniform and badge and carrying a clipboard. The Robertsons all streamed out of the shed to see who he was, and Mallory and the others followed. He was Hispanic, with olive skin, curly black hair, and a wispy beard that looked more accidental than intentional. He was wearing a nameplate that read Arsenio Santiago.

"Good morning," he said. He seemed friendly and a bit uncomfortable. "I'm looking for David Robertson?"

"That's me," Pete's uncle said, stepping

forward.

"I'm very sorry, Mr. Robertson," Santiago said. "I'm with the State, and you're going to have to stop selling Robertsons' Remedies. I'm here to seal off the door to your shop."

"What?" Pete's uncle said. "What in the world – ?"

"As you know, we've gotten complaints," Santiago said, "and we have to investigate. I'm very sorry. I know this comes as a shock. I really hate this part of my job, telling a small business owner like you – . Of course you'll have an opportunity to protest this action, but at the moment there's nothing I can do. I need to close off the shop. You're instructed not to sell any more supplements of any kind – not in person and not by mail order. I have a number of papers I'll have to ask you to sign."

He thrust the clipboard at Mr. Robertson who recoiled as if he'd been offered a poisonous snake.

"I won't sign anything without my lawyer's advice," he said. "But how can you close us down? You can see for yourself we sell Golden Globe citrus out of the same shop, and we have customers who stop by all the time."

"I'm sorry," Santiago said. "I sympathize."

"All sorts of people drive in, some from quite a distance. We can't disappoint them. We've actually had quite a few famous people as customers. My dad started the grove, and he sold to Buck Owens and Merle Haggard. We're really quite an institution in Bakersfield."

"Congratulations!" Santiago said. "I love country music. I'm a regular at the Roundup. I go there almost every night."

The Roundup, Mallory thought. That was the place Cueball had mentioned.

"Listen," Santiago went on. "I'll do everything in my power to help you. I feel especially bad when it's the little guys like you who suffer. It would be much easier on me if I only had to slap citations on rich guys like your next-door neighbor. Franklin Weaver owns half the town of Bakersfield! And he thinks he owns the other half as well – together with all the people who live there. I'd love to get him. But today, I'm sorry to say, I don't have any excuse to do that."

Arsenio Santiago walked over to the shed and lowered the garage-type door. On it he fastened a large white sign that said in big black letters Closed By Order Of The California Rapid Response Health And Safety Commission. He'd signed it Arsenio Santiago, Commissioner, at the bottom. Then he took from his pocket what looked like yellow police tape and he stretched it from one end of the shed to the other.

David Robertson looked very pale to Mallory. Lilliana had come to stand next to him, and both Estevan and Gabriella huddled close, as if they were under physical threat. In fact, Mallory thought, it was as if their property had been subjected to a small invasion.

"I'm really very sorry, Mr. Robertson," Arsenio Santiago said. "The Commission will be in touch in two or three weeks – "

"Two or three weeks!" David Robertson exploded.

Santiago nodded. "Then you can file an appeal. I'll leave these papers with you," he said, taking the clipboard back and giving Pete's uncle the papers it contained. "In the meantime, have a good day." He nodded cordially to the assemblage, got into his official-looking car, and drove away.

"Have a good day?" Pete said.

Everyone stood stock still, as if they'd been frozen. Mallory felt sick to her stomach that such a nice family had just been treated so badly by what seemed a totally inflexible – not to mention deeply stupid – system. Why should

Dave and Lilliana Robertson wait two or three weeks to find out why the state had shut them down?

Breaking the silence, Jupiter said, "That man certainly didn't seem to like your next-door neighbor. I wonder if part of his job involves inspecting the rides at the amusement park. Maybe that's the source of the hostility between him and Franklin Weaver."

"He did seem to be sorry," Lilliana said. "That's something. At least he wasn't nasty."

"No, that's true," David said. "And he told us he'd do everything he could to help us. Maybe there are some people who do this sort of thing who still have a heart in their chests."

Mallory couldn't disagree. Arsenio Santiago *had* seemed to regret what he'd been sent to do. In fact, he'd seemed really sympathetic. Maybe there was a way he actually *could* help so that the Robertsons could get back in business sooner than three weeks.

Still, as soon as she'd thought that, she found herself remembering the story Wally had told about the California DMV. He'd said that bureaucracies attract the worst kind of people, and that if they couldn't be bureaucrats, maybe they'd be vicious killers. He'd been half-kidding, but less than twenty-four hours later, Mallory had listened to Cueball say that he and his friends were  big on being able to make their own decisions without any meddling from stupid bureaucrats or lying politicians – and all of a sudden Mallory was overtaken by the very same feeling that Bob had reported feeling the day before.

Maybe the Robertsons' situation would take more tools to solve than The Three Investigators were carrying in their tool-kit. In addition, Mallory felt just plain angry that a country like America – a country with so many interesting facets and fascinating people – would be subject to so much unnecessary oversight from power-hungry idiots. She couldn't help but hope that Jupiter's mighty brain would somehow rise to the occasion.

## 4

## Jupiter Gets To Work

**It** was over an hour later, and although Jupiter had hinted broadly any number of times that The Three Investigators' time in Bakersfield was limited, and that the main reason they had come today was not to eat lunch but to investigate a crime, so far Lilliana Robertson had been so determined to be a good hostess to her nephew and his friends that Jupiter hadn't been able to ask a single substantive question about the actual matters at hand.

Granted, as soon as the family and its guests had entered the Robertsons' house after Arsenio Santiago had departed, Mr. Robertson had called his lawyer in Bakersfield and made an appointment to meet with him immediately after lunch. He had also mentioned that four weeks before – about the time he'd finally called on one of the county agricultural extension agents to help him figure out what was killing the trees – he'd gotten his first call from the Health and Safety Commission. The woman he'd spoken to had told him there had been several complaints from people who had bought the San Joaquin Valley Supplement. They'd said it had irritated their stomachs so badly they'd had pains for days.

From what Jupiter gathered, there had been no complaints before – and although the Robertson family made all of its lotions and unguents right there in one of their sheds, the supplements, including the one at issue, were all made by a facility in Fresno, which also fulfilled all the online orders for Robertsons' Remedies.

The Robertsons also sold their supplements in the shop and through selected retailers, but most of their business was online, and everything was sent from Fresno, with Robertsons' Remedies stickers.

It seemed likely to Jupiter that Santiago had already notified the Fresno facility, as well as any local stores that carried the supplements. Although he tried to control his impatience to know more, it occurred to him that perhaps one batch of the targeted supplement had gotten polluted, somehow, at the factory.

At last, the meal was almost over, and Jupiter was able to ask Dave Robertson what, if anything, he had done after the first call from the Health and Safety Commission.

"Well, as it turns out, one of the ingredients in the supplement is a bioflavonoid called quercetin and one is the mineral zinc. Both are excellent boosts to the immune system, but both of them can occasionally irritate peoples' stomachs. So we thought maybe people were taking too much, or taking the capsules on an empty stomach. Even so, we wanted to have a random batch tested by the same lab that tested our soil sample. But the Commission arranged for its own test – which came back saying that the supplement *had* been polluted."

"With what?" Jupiter asked.

"They refused to say," Mr. Robertson said. "The papers they sent through the mail didn't specify. I'm sure that all of this can be sorted out in time, but we really don't have time. We have bills that come due every single month. And even though the grove can probably survive because of our mail order citrus business, it's still the worst kind of publicity, isn't it? I mean, would you buy your oranges from some place that had been closed down by the Health and Safety Commission?"

"Probably not," Jupiter said.

"But Robertsons' Remedies? That part of our business won't survive for more than a month if we're not allowed to sell either from our shop or from the Fresno place."

"Do you have any enemies?" Jupiter asked.

"Hardly," Mrs. Robertson said.

"None that we know of, anyway," Mr. Robertson clarified.

"Do you think that we could see the sales records for the San Joaquin Valley supplement for the last six months or so?" Jupiter asked.

"Certainly," Mrs. Robertson said, "but it'll take a while for Gabriella and me to get them all together. One of us will make a PDF and send it to you by e-mail."

"That would be fine," Jupiter said. "While you're at it, perhaps you could also send us a list of the people you regularly sell your citrus fruit to. It's just a stab in the dark, but we have to start somewhere."

"I agree," Mrs. Robertson said. "But let's have dessert first. Please let's not talk about our problems again until afterwards."

Jupiter could see little sense in doing that, since one of the things he wanted to discover was the history of the Robertsons' citrus grove, so he was pleased when Mallory asked why it was called the Golden Globe.

For the first time since Arsenio Santiago had showed up on his property, Mr. Robertson actually smiled. "My dad thought it would be a great gimmick" he said. "He bought the grove about five years after the Golden Globe Awards started in 1943, by which time a lot of newspaper guys had started to dress up their prose by calling navel oranges 'golden globes.' And one of the ways my father tried to get regular repeat customers was by asking anyone famous who stopped by to have their picture taken holding an orange.

"I mentioned Buck Owens and Merle Haggard earlier," Pete's uncle continued. "There was also Frank Gifford, the All-American and pro football player and sports commentator, and a bunch of other sports figures, both national and local, and a whole lot of local musicians and athletes. In fact we actually have a couple of celebrities right now who get their oranges once a month from us. Most of them just stopped by and liked the fruit so much they signed up for a subscription. I never had the courage to ask the recent ones to pose for a picture. My dad had no shame."

"He was a good salesman," Wally said, "and he certainly had plenty of cheek."

"Where are all the pictures now?" Mallory asked.

"They were hanging on the walls of the shop," Mr. Robertson said. "But when we renovated a few years ago, we put all of them in the barn. I'm not sure that was such a good idea. Even if Buck Owens and Merle Haggard and their bands seem a bit dated, they're still an important part of Bakersfield's history. That's what I said to Mr. Santiago."

"He certainly knew who they were," Jupiter said.

"Yes, he did," Mr. Robertson said. "But then he hangs out at the Roundup."

Jupiter himself wasn't at all sure who Merle Haggard and Buck Owens were, but he was starting to get the picture as Mr. and Mrs. Robertson talked at length about Bakersfield's history as a working class city, and about the San Joaquin Valley's history of western migration from Oklahoma and Arkansas. As a refuge for farmers fleeing the Dust Bowl, it had long had a love of country western music.

"I was never really a fan," Wally said to Pete's uncle. "But your father sure loved country western. He used to like to go to the General Store in Lindsay, which had a jukebox. He'd sit around on a fruit crate and hope someone would put a nickel or a dime in the box. I was just reminded of all that because the General Store was owned by the father of a kid we went to school with – a kid named Franklin

Weaver, just like the guy who Arsenio Santiago disliked so much.

"We used to call the kid we went to school with 'Two,' because he was Franklin Weaver II, and he was too obnoxious. His father who owned the General Store was One. The first Franklin Weaver made a great success of that store. He sold just about everything, but his big draw was oranges. He sold navels and Valencias and mandarins at rock bottom prices, undercutting everyone around. That, and the jukebox. That's why people went to Weaver's General Store."

Although Jupiter couldn't have said exactly why, he was starting to get strangely interested in this story. When Wally had asked if he could come on this expedition, Jupiter hadn't been certain exactly what he might be able to contribute to the investigation. But he'd had a funny feeling that if he did come to the Robertsons with them, some sort of contribution would be forthcoming – and maybe this was it.

Wally took a deep breath and went on.

"Frankie Weaver – that's what everyone but me and Charlie called him – was – . Well, there are words for who he was but I shouldn't use them in polite company. He could make you want to throttle his skinny little neck in sixty seconds. Fifty on a good day," Wally said. "His father was all right, but Two was a peckerhead if you know what I mean. He hated Charlie and me so much that one time he told us he'd happily spend his whole life making sure he ruined ours!"

Everyone laughed at what Jupiter supposed was another bit of Wally's hyperbole, but he couldn't help but think that it was also as good a definition of an enemy as he'd ever heard.

"Why did he hate you so much?" Pete asked.

"Because we were movie stars and he wasn't," Wally said.

Everyone laughed again.

"No, really," Wally said. "They filmed part of the end of John Ford's *The Grapes of Wrath* near Bakersfield, at a government camp called Weedpatch. This was late fall, 1939. Charlie and I were both 15, working for the Central California Ice Company, when the word went around the high school that they were looking for extras for a crowd scene in the movie. Some would get a small speaking part, shouting things out from the crowd. Everyone wanted a part.

"Including Two, Frankie Weaver himself," Wally went on. "Frankie just assumed that because of who his daddy was and because he was rich and a big wheel in high school, he'd naturally be picked. He made merciless fun of Charlie and me for even thinking we had a chance. But of course what he didn't understand was that the casting director was looking for Okies – kids who looked the part, working class boys. When we got cast and he didn't, that's when he said that thing about ruining our lives."

"We all saw that movie in eighth grade," Pete said, "and I didn't see you in it."

"Well, Pete," Wally said. "I was a little younger then. I still had all my hair, for one thing."

"Geez," Pete said. "Of course."

"I never saw Two again after I came back from the war. But I remember Charlie telling me that his father – the one who owned the General Store – died pretty young. He said Frankie moved to Bakersfield and bought himself a department store. Charlie would run into him from time to time, and he told me Two hadn't changed. Still a peckerhead.

"But he was also very successful, from what Charlie told me. He just hoovered up money. He got married and had a family but he never seemed to have gotten around to ruining our lives! Anyway, when we passed the sign for the Citrus and Carnival Ranch, and I saw that god-awful name Franklin Weaver, I wondered for a moment if that could be Two's son. But then I thought no, that couldn't be. Because he would have been Franklin Weaver III – and no son of Two would ever leave those Roman numerals off his name."

Wally had been talking so quickly that no one had had a chance to say a word, and Jupiter had been watching Lilliana and David Robertsons' faces which had become more and more animated as they listened.

"But his name *is* Franklin Weaver III!" Lillian said as soon as Wally was quiet. Wally, Pete, Bob, and Mallory looked at her in amazement. "I don't think everyone knows that," she went on, "but we do. About five years ago, not long after Weaver bought the neighboring grove, I ambled down to the mailbox on the highway and there was a formal offer to buy our orchard. You could have knocked me over with a feather.

"Our place wasn't on the market, of course, and so this offer just came out of the blue. We had absolutely no desire to sell the place, and I was so shocked that I'll never forget that signature across the bottom of the offer – Franklin Weaver III."

"What happened?" Jupiter asked, his voice surprisingly urgent.

"The contract was time-sensitive," Mr. Robertson said. "It expired in forty-eight hours if we didn't accept it. So we didn't accept it, and it expired."

"We took it to our lawyer," Mrs. Robertson said. "It was a valid offer, he told us, and for a bit more than market value. We've had almost nothing to do with Mr. Weaver in the time since, though he did make a strong impression with that piece of paper."

"So he hasn't been a good neighbor?" Mallory asked.

"I can't say he's been a bad neighbor," Mr. Robertson said. "Of course we were upset when the rides went in, but we couldn't do anything about that. We really don't know very much about him at all. Still, it seemed odd to us that he used those acres to build an amusement park instead of planting orange trees, as most anyone else would have done."

"We don't know anything about his personal life," Mrs. Robertson said, "but we sort of assume that he must like children. Because of all the rides. Anyway, it turned out that his amusement park was a blessing in disguise. At the time, it took away almost all our pick-straight-from-the-tree customers, but if that hadn't happened, we'd never have started Robertsons' Remedies, and that has been great for us — not only in terms of the business but in terms of us working together as a family. At least until this Health and Safety Commission came along."

"And that amusement park hasn't been all bad for us, either," Mr. Robertson said. "In fact, Mateo — you haven't met him yet, but he's our oldest — is actually working there this summer. He's there right now, and he likes his job. I don't think he's had anything to do with Franklin Weaver, but he seems to like the man who runs the place. He told us he was so sorry to miss seeing you today, Pete."

"Maybe we'll be back," Pete said.

"Anyway," Mrs. Robertson said to Wally, "I bet our next-door neighbor *is* the son of Franklin II. But he's no doubt considerably better than his father was. He's given the children who live around here a water slide and a Ferris wheel and a Tilt-A-Whirl, and he really charges very little to get in. It's almost as if he's doing it as a service and not to make money at all."

"You forgot to tell them about him coming by in the winter," Gabriella said.

Mrs. Robertson looked at her daughter for a moment as though she were trying to remember. "That's right!" she said. "He dropped by unannounced, for the first and only time since he bought his place. When was it, Gabriella?"

"February," Gabriella said.

"You tell them, Gabby. You and Mateo are the ones who met him," Mr. Robertson said.

Gabriella nodded. "You and Mom had gone to town with Estevan. Well, he drove in and came into the shed and introduced himself. He spent a long time looking around, and he finally bought some soap and some lip balm. Then he spent time reading through that little book we have on a chain by the Valley supplement, with all the testimonials from people who said it kept them from getting sick, and not just with the fever but with colds or the flu or whatever.

"A couple of people said they'd never been so healthy in their lives as they've been since they started taking it. Mr. Weaver said he was very impressed, and that it was great we sold a product that helped with such a difficult disease. And he bought ten whole bottles!"

Though the Robertsons didn't seem to think much of this other than the fact that they'd had a larger than normal sale, Jupiter took notice in a different way. The Robertsons had had few dealings with this Franklin Weaver III, but the ones they'd had were odd. First he had offered to buy their entire operation, and then five years later he had dropped by and supported their new business. Perhaps Weaver and the Citrus and Carnival Ranch ought to be investigated.

Because his land bordered theirs, someone from his property could easily have gotten to those dying orange trees. And the words with which his father had menaced David Robertsons' father and Wally – that he'd happily spend his whole life ruining theirs – didn't sound like the usual threat. Long-held grudges were a dark and poisonous force, festering unseen.

Nevertheless Frankie Weaver, a.k.a. Two, had uttered this imprecation when he'd been a frustrated teenager, and he might well have quickly forgotten it as he rose in business. Besides, the current Franklin Weaver was that man's son, and *he* had no grudge against the Robertsons.

But why had Weaver stopped in unannounced five months ago and bought ten whole bottles of the San Joaquin Valley supplement? That seemed most curious of all to Jupiter. Ten bottles was a lot, and at the moment Jupiter couldn't think of a good reason why one customer would buy that many at one time.

Though he didn't imagine that Weaver was on the premises of his carnival at the moment, Jupiter thought it might be a good idea to stop by and talk to Pete's cousin Mateo, and maybe to the manager, to see what they had to say about their boss.

Mr. Robertson glanced at his watch. "Lilli, this was delicious," he said to his wife. "I'm sorry I have to run. But if I don't leave soon, I'll be late for my appointment at the lawyer's. Wally, I don't know when I'll be back, so let me say goodbye now. I'm so glad you came over to visit us. Please come again."

"Thank you, David," Wally said. "I surely will."

"The rest of you, too, of course," Mr. Robertson said. He kissed his wife on the cheek and waved goodbye as he left.

Pete jumped to his feet. "Let us clean up, Aunt Lilli," he said.

"No," his aunt said. "You're here for

such a short time, we'll clean up after you leave. But let us show you the dying orange trees before you go. Wally, it's quite a ways. Are you game?"

"I think I'll have a little rest after that marvelous meal," Wally said. "Just park me in a chair outside in the shade."

Jupiter had never been in an orange grove before. The quiet was amazing. Though there was a slight breeze, it didn't seem to rustle the leaves. Most of the trees they passed were navel orange trees, whose crop had passed, though a few unpicked shriveling oranges hung in the branches or had dropped to the ground under them. But the Valencia trees were still so heavy with fruit Jupiter couldn't quite believe the branches could hold the weight. The oranges were indeed golden globes, shining in the sun, each tree brightly decorated and jaunty. The rinds' oils hung in the air. Everything smelled like orange.

Then up ahead Jupiter saw a patch of ground that looked as though it had been blasted. A grid of twenty-five trees stood out from the rest. Their leaves were brown and twisted, curled in on themselves. In the midst of the grove's lushness, they were shocking. He could see that everyone with him found the experience upsetting. The others stood quietly as Jupiter inspected the area, his hands clasped behind his back. Every now and then he hunkered down and scratched at the dust.

"When you called in the agricultural agent to take soil samples, did you notice anything unusual?" Jupiter asked. "Any signs of salt? Of of whoever did this?"

"Not really," Mrs. Robertson said. "But we did find one of those plastic tubes you hammer into the ground to fertilize the trees' roots."

"Did you send that to the lab as well?" Jupiter asked.

"No," Mrs. Robertson said. "We just threw it out. It looked like ones we'd used in the past. We assumed it was just one of our old ones."

"Thank you," he said. "I'm very sorry about the trees. They're not a pretty sight."

He looked at his watch. It was getting on toward mid-afternoon and they ought to call Worthington. He thought they'd discovered all they could for the moment at the Golden Globe Citrus Grove.

Soon they were all saying goodbye to Pete's aunt and cousins and thanking them again for lunch.

"I'm sorry the circumstances were so unpleasant," Pete's aunt said. "Do come back and see us again soon, all of you."

She turned to Pete. "But especially you. Give your mother a big hug and a kiss from me."

"I will, Aunt Lilli," Pete said. "Thanks again."

From this, Jupiter gathered that neither Pete nor his Aunt Lilli understood yet that Jupiter had truly committed to looking into the Robertsons' problems. But he had. As Worthington drove down the dirt road leading back to the highway, Jupiter sat next to Pete again, in the third seat. He watched as Pete kept turning to look back at his aunt and uncle's house. Finally he settled down in his seat, looking seriously deflated.

"Thanks a lot," Pete said. "All of you. Really. I appreciate your coming today. And thanks for being so nice about something that looks so hopeless."

"That's not like you at all," Mallory said. "Where's the fighting spirit?"

"I left it back with those dead trees," Pete said. "I don't think I've ever seen anything so depressing. Who could have done such a thing? Salt! It could be anybody. And why? For kicks?" Pete said. "And what about the Health and Safety Commission?"

"One thing at a time," Jupiter said.

"I know everyone was sort of hoping we might check out the carnival," Pete said, "but I'm sure no one's in the mood after what just happened."

"On the contrary," Jupiter said. "I think we very much ought to see this amusement park."

"What?" Pete said, astounded. "But you don't even *like* amusement parks."

"That may be true," Jupiter said, with a slight smile. "But I think I may like this one. And not just because I want to talk with your cousin Mateo, but also because I think Franklin Weaver the Third and his operation may be worth a very close look."

## 5

## A Haunted History

**P**ete was often surprised by Jupiter, but rarely so completely. Ever since Pete had sprung the news to his friends about the promise Bob had made to his mother the day before, he'd been regretting not standing up to her better when he'd still had the chance. That look of triumph she'd given him when she got off the phone with Aunt Lilli and told him that the Robertsons' trees had been purposely poisoned had made it hard to think straight, but even so, he could have drawn back from this whole hopeless case before he dragged Jupiter and Mallory into it.

Up to now, he'd been assuming that they hadn't really wanted to come to Bakersfield in the first place. In fact, Pete had supposed that Jupiter in particular would be eager to get back to Rocky Beach – yet here he was, not only delaying their return, but urging them to go to a place you'd usually have to drag him to.

"You really want to investigate?" Pete asked. "You think you may have discovered something?" He felt a surge of hope.

Jupiter shrugged. "There's no way of knowing yet," he said. "But there are several items of note."

"Like what?" Pete said.

"When we saw the dead trees," Jupiter asked, "who was the closest neighbor?"

"Franklin Weaver," Bob said. "You think he – "

"Just a coincidence perhaps," Jupiter said. "Then there's the threat his father made."

"About ruining my life," Wally said. "And Charlie's."

"And didn't you think it was odd that Mr. Weaver bought ten bottles of the San Joaquin Valley supplement?" Jupiter asked. "What was he going to do with all of those?"

"Maybe he wanted to stock up," Pete said. "Maybe he wanted to hand them out to the people who worked for him, to keep them from getting sick."

"Possibly," Jupiter said. "But it did seem like a large purchase."

By now, Worthington had turned under the sign for the Citrus and Carnival Ranch, hard on the heels of another car filled with eager children. Worthington dropped back to avoid the clouds of dust kicked up by the vehicle's wheels, then parked among a host of other cars in a gravel parking lot.

Pete took a deep breath and looked around him. The park had a chain link fence surrounding it, and a gaudy arched entrance, hung with streamers, where the ticket booth was. Flashy red pennants hung on strings and colorful banners proclaimed the names of all the games of chance on the midway. The air smelled of popcorn and cotton candy. Bright carnival music, fast-tempo'd, filled with horns, blared from loudspeakers. Most of the rides seemed to have their own music as well, and the various sounds created a pleasant cacophony. The midway was crowded with boys and girls lined up to try their luck, shooting at tin ducks, pitching pennies, throwing balls at small clown figures, trying to knock them over.

Right in the middle, the Ferris wheel stood. With the Valley being so flat, you could probably see all the way to Fresno and over to the foothills of the coastal range to the west, Pete thought.

"Look!" Bob said. "Bumper cars!"

The biggest lines were for the roller coasters. Pete saw that there were two of them, both constructed of wooden scaffolding with steel tracks that twisted through sharp turns, dipped and banked and dropped steeply. The Cyclotron had long sinuous carts that held eight or ten riders, but the other, The Nemesis, had carts that held just two, side by side. Both of them looked fantastic, but only the Cyclotron seemed to be operating – and anyway, what Pete was actually looking for was a glimpse of his cousin Mateo. If Jupiter wanted to meet and talk with him for some Jupiterish reason, then Pete would have to find him first.

To do that, they needed to buy tickets, but when Wally's turn came, he demurred.

"I think I'll try to persuade my friend Worthington to accompany me to that nice air-conditioned restaurant I saw when we were driving in – for a glass of something with lots of ice." He looked at Worthington hopefully.

"Certainly, you old codger," Worthington said. "Let's make tracks." He turned to Pete and the others. "Come find us when you're ready to head back." He took Wally's arm and they were off.

As if he'd been reading Pete's thoughts – "All right," Jupiter said. "Time to find Mateo." But before Pete could even get started in his search, a gaggle of kids came barreling down the fairway. One of them, trying to get in front, didn't watch where he was going and bumped into Pete. He tumbled in the dirt at his feet.

Pete reached down and hoisted the boy up. He was about six or seven, hot and sweaty, and he looked uncertain and embarrassed. Pete grabbed him by the shoulders. "Are you O.K.?" he asked.

The boy nodded, expecting to be yelled at. "Sorry," he said.

"That's all right," Pete said. "No harm done." He tousled the kid's hair and pushed him in the direction of his friends. "Go on then," he said. "Watch where you're running."

The kid grinned at him and ran off yelling to join his friends. As Pete watched him go, his mind went back to the kid he and Bob had seen in downtown Rocky Beach – the one who had managed to drop a whole piano.

Of course, he'd been a good deal older than *this* kid, but kids in general were prone to accidents, he thought, and there was really nothing you could do about it but let them learn from their own experience. You couldn't wrap people up in bubble wrap. Yet that was just what all these health and safety commissions and departments seemed to think you *could* do. It was a really stupid thing to think.

Just then he caught sight of Mateo, hurrying with a toolbox toward an older man lying on his back near the scaffolding that seemed to hold the main motor of The Nemesis. There was a sign by the entrance that read "Closed for Repairs."

Weirdly enough, "nemesis" was a word Pete actually knew. His soccer coach at Rocky Beach High was always calling this or that potential opponent a "nemesis." According to him, the word meant a long-standing rival or an enemy – though he also sometimes used it to refer to a balance beam he insisted his players practice on. Why anyone would call a roller-coaster *that* was a mystery to Pete. Weren't roller-coasters supposed to be fun?

Mateo looked the same as ever – tall and fit, broad shouldered, quick on his feet. He'd cut his black hair short and was growing a little goatee.

"Mateo!" Pete shouted, waving.

His cousin stopped running and scanned the crowd to see who had called his name. When he saw Pete waving, he grinned. "Pete!" he yelled. "I thought I wasn't going to get to see you today!"

Pete and the others hurried over. Pete and Mateo hugged, slapping one another on the back. Pete had always admired his older cousin and had literally looked up to him. But now he was staring Mateo right in the eyes.

"Wow!" Mateo said. "You've gotten so big! I pity your opponents on the soccer field."

"You look great!" Pete said. "But what's this?" He reached out and tugged on the goatee.

Mateo laughed. "Just an experiment," he said. "Don't go giving me grief. My parents give me enough already."

Pete turned to his friends and introduced them. They all shook hands. "Welcome to the carnival!" Mateo said. "It's actually a pretty fun place – even if it *did* steal half my family's business. Not that *it* did that, of course. Franklin Weaver the Third did. And I shouldn't call it stealing, really. It was only business."

"I'm sorry for your family's troubles," Jupiter said.

Mateo looked at Jupiter curiously. "Why?" he asked. "Do you know something I don't?"

Pete nodded. "Just after we got up here, this guy drove in and closed down your farm stand. He shut the door and posted a sign and stretched that yellow tape across the front. He was from some place called the California Rapid Response Health and Safety Commission. Did I remember it right, Jupe?"

Jupiter nodded.

"The same crew that sent those papers to my dad about some supposed problem with the San Joaquin Valley supplement," Mateo said.

"Your mother said that you're the one who thought that supplement up," Mallory said.

"Yes," Mateo said. It was clear that he was quite upset that the problem was with his own brainchild. "Did you catch the guy's name?" he asked.

"Arsenio Santiago," Pete said. "He seemed like a decent guy. Very apologetic."

"Santiago, huh?" Mateo said. "He's the guy who does spot checks on the rides here. He came by a few days ago and he found a problem with The Nemesis. Or said he did. I personally couldn't see what the fuss was about. The ride has been working fine. But you're right. He does seem decent – or at least semi-decent – and Billy and I are doing what he told us to now."

He nodded toward the man over by The Nemesis.

"Billy?" Jupiter asked.

"Billy Taylor," Mateo said. "He's my

boss. I mean, Mr. Weaver is my real boss, but Billy is the carnival manager. Billy hired me, and he runs the whole place. I guess he's an old friend of Mr. Weaver's."

"He not only runs things," Pete said. "He fixes things too?"

"He's a mechanical wizard," Mateo said. "He was born in Oildale, about five miles northeast of Bakersfield, and he worked most of his life in the oil fields. He still loves to fix things. He's also great with the kids. Come on. I'll introduce you. Besides I need to get these tools to him." He started walking over toward The Nemesis.

Pete and the others followed. Billy Taylor was on his back on the ground, his head and torso out of view behind some painted lattice that shielded the roller coaster's mechanicals. "Is that you, Mateo?" he called out. "I was wondering when you'd show up."

"I just ran into my cousin," Mateo said. "Come on out for a sec."

Billy Taylor wiggled out from under the enclosure and sat up. His hands and forearms were dark with grease, and he had a big smear across his forehead. His hair was almost totally gray and he had a small paunch. But he looked rugged and sunburned and he was very friendly as he got to his feet.

"This is my cousin Pete," Mateo said, "and his friends Mallory, Bob, and Jupiter."

"I'm pleased to meet you," Billy Taylor said, grinning. "You'll pardon me if I don't shake hands. How do you like the place?"

"We actually just got here, Mr. Taylor," Jupiter said, "but everything seems very festive."

"Don't Mr. Taylor me," he said. "Call me Billy. Everyone else does. How old are you four anyway? What grade are you in?"

"We'll be juniors in the fall," Pete said.

"Good for you," Billy said. "You keep at it. It's important to get a high school diploma. A lot of the kids I hire for the summer are just waiting to drop out. Don't be like them. Not having a high school education will hurt you in the long run."

"We agree," Jupiter said. "We all intend to go on to − "

"I might have gone to college," Billy Taylor said, "but the Vietnam War got in the way. I graduated in 1971 but in working class families like mine, it would have been considered unpatriotic to try to get out of serving. And when I got back, I had to find a job. Will you excuse me if I get back to work while I talk?"

"Sure," Pete said. "Don't let us bother you."

He watched as Billy Taylor rummaged in the tool box, came up with a big red-handled screwdriver, and with a few deft movements, unscrewed and removed the lattice so he could better get at the roller coaster's motor. He removed the motor's housing and started tinkering with some internal mechanism. He had the same easy confidence with his hands that Pete's father had. After watching him work for a while, Jupiter asked how he had gotten his job managing the amusement park.

"Well," he said, "I came out here one afternoon with two of my sons and their kids. And who did I run into but Franklin Weaver The Third? We went to school together, though we ran with different crowds. He and I were always friendly, though. We were both born in 1952, though he grew up in a neighborhood a lot ritzier than Oildale. He went to college, too – locally, at Bakersfield State. It had just opened when Franklin started there. I know he never joined up or got drafted, I don't know why.

"I was away a lot, in the oil business," he continued, "and I hardly ever ran into Franklin.

But that day we got to talking, and he told me he was looking to hire a new manager, and I got the job. Of course, it doesn't pay all that much – Franklin always did pinch a nickel until it shrieked – but I enjoy it, and I get to work with rapscallions like Mateo here."

Mateo grinned at that.

"But I have to say," Billy went on, "I don't really understand Franklin. After all, we're both over seventy, and at our age, money isn't really that important any more. But old Franklin can't relax. He's got his finger in every pie in Bakersfield." He laughed. "He takes chances when it comes to money, but none in real life – not since he was a kid."

"Why's that?" Pete asked.

"Well, I'm just an armchair psychologist," Billy said, turning his attention back to the motor. "But when we were about ten, I guess, there was a huge dust storm in Bakersfield, and a whole lot of people came down sick with Valley fever. Franklin got it, and though it didn't hurt him too bad, afterwards he was a lot more cautious on the playground – maybe because his granddad had died of the fever, I don't know.

"A lot of us kids did crazy stuff – racing hot rods, playing chicken in the rail yard – but

Franklin never did." Billy shook his head in wonder. "And now he owns two roller coasters! Of course, he never goes on them. Me neither! I was daring all my life, but all those years of hard labor in the oil fields have given me a bum ticker."

"That's terrible," Pete said.

"Oh, don't go feeling sorry for me," Billy said. "I've been on plenty of roller coasters – and worse! – when I was younger. But my grandkids love them, and so do Franklin's. Can you believe there's a Franklin Weaver the Fifth?"

He turned toward Pete and the others with a wry smile. "He thinks he's an English king or something!" he chortled. "Anyway, we both have grandsons who just turned thirteen and they're so excited to get to ride The Nemesis."

"Why is that?" Jupiter asked. "Can't anyone ride it?"

Billy Taylor shook his head. "Only teenagers. Between 13 and 19. We make them show ID. They love it. And three nights a week – we call them Nemesis Nights – everything else in the carnival's closed except The Nemesis, and the teenagers come to ride it in the dark. No lights, only the stars overhead – and the moon if they're lucky!"

"Wow!" Pete said. "That sounds pretty cool."

"And we make it even cooler," Mateo said. "The carts are just for two people, so most of them are couples. And there's a spot where whoever's controlling the ride stops the cart on a hairpin turn. They're thrown into one another's arms, screaming and laughing. Though it's plenty scary, I can tell you. I've been on it."

"Not only has he been on it," Billy said. "Now he's the one who runs the monster on Nemesis Nights."

"How do you run it without any lights on?" Mallory asked.

"I have a big flashlight with a high-powered beam," Mateo said, "so I can buckle the people in the right way and see the controls. And there's a bit of light pollution from Bakersfield. But even so, it's amazing how dark it gets. It's totally different riding a roller coaster in the dark. I have to make sure I stop the cart at just the right place or someone could get badly hurt."

"Someone actually did, once," Billy said. "Not here, but in its original location in Fresno. One of the carts went whizzing right off –

broke its cables and plummeted straight to the ground."

Jeez, Pete thought. Just like that piano.

"Yup," Billy continued, nodding. "It just smashed there, with two people in it. One was killed and one was badly hurt. That's why it's called The Nemesis now – because Franklin Weaver thought it would be a good gimmick to advertise the roller-coaster as haunted by the ghost of the guy who was killed on it."

He shook his head a bit disapprovingly. "He was right, too. A lot of the kids who love it claim it *is* haunted. That they can sometimes hear the couple who crashed to the ground, screaming!"

"Really *screaming*?" asked Pete.

"Of course not really screaming," said Jupiter. "Hmmm. I would have thought this new Health and Safety Commission would have insisted the ride be dismantled, right there in Fresno."

"I know what you mean," said Billy. "But this was years ago, and that Commission hadn't been formed yet. The Fresno amusement park went out of business after the accident, but the county allowed the owner to sell off all its different parts."

"And the whole thing was re-built when it

arrived here," said Mateo. "Though it only became a big success when Franklin Weaver came up with the idea of Nemesis Nights for teenagers."

"Have you ever met Mr. Weaver?" asked Jupiter.

"Oh, yes!" said Mateo. "Not lots of times, but a couple. And, of course, he was the one who actually hired me."

Jupiter suddenly looked like a terrier who had spotted a rat, Pete thought.

"I thought Billy was the manager," Jupiter said, as casually as he could manage – which didn't seem all that casually to Pete. "Didn't you say you hired the teenage summer workers?" he asked Billy.

"Normally, I do," Billy said, picking up a rag and wiping oil off his hands. "But for some strange reason Franklin didn't like the guy I wanted to hire to run Nemesis Nights. He said he'd met Mateo when he'd stopped in at his family's farm stand and shop, and that he had struck him as really responsible. Also, since he lived right next door, he could probably pinch-hit if he needed  to. He'd be here in no time at all, Franklin said."

"I haven't had to do that," said Mateo. "But though I wasn't all that wild about the idea of working here this summer, when I met Franklin Weaver, he told me that if I did a good job, and nothing bad happened on The Nemesis, he'd give me a bonus of $2000 at the end of the summer."

"You're kidding!" said Pete. "That's a lot of money!"

"It really is," said Mateo. "Well, listen. I'd love to talk some more, but I've got to get back to work now. So does Billy. Is there any chance you'll be coming back soon?"

At this, Pete, Bob and Mallory all looked at Jupiter.

"I'd say there's an excellent chance," he said.

They said goodbye and headed out the main gate and down past the parking area. Pete had a lot of questions he wanted answered, but when he started to ask them, Jupiter said he needed to think.

Then, just as they were getting to the restaurant, a white panel truck pulled up by the entrance. On its side had been painted the words "Speedy Gonzales Courier Service – We Get Your Package There Yesterday!" There was a picture of a cartoon mouse wearing a yellow sombrero, white shirt and trousers, and a red kerchief. A cartoon bubble read "Más rápido!" A man jumped out of the truck wearing a white uniform and a red kerchief and went into the restaurant.

Pete and the others followed. As Pete passed the cash register, the courier was handing a package to the woman behind it. Wally and Worthington were sitting at the counter talking amiably. "Hi, Wally!" Pete called. "Did you miss us?"

"Miss you?" Wally said. "I've been bereft."

Pete often thought that Wally's vocabulary was too big.

They all hustled to the car and were soon back on the road to Rocky Beach.

"So did you guys have a good time?" Mallory asked Worthington.

"Yes, we actually did," Worthington said. "The waitress who served us – Dotty – is a big fan of country western music. She told us about a bar in Bakersfield that has great live music and line and square and swing dancing. Sawdust and peanut shells on the floor. Beer in big tall glasses. Her sister Kitty works in the restaurant attached to it."

"Is the bar called the Roundup?" Pete asked.

"How on earth did you know?" Worthington asked.

"My uncle mentioned it earlier," Pete said.

"It seems Dotty goes there a lot," Worthington said. "It's one of those places that attracts people from all walks of life – rich people and not-so-rich people like her, professional types and blue-collar workers. She said she'd even seen a famous movie star there. She couldn't remember his name or how she knew him, but he was very handsome and young, and she thought he was Indian."

"Indian from India?" Mallory asked.

"Yes," Worthington said. "I couldn't help wondering if it could have been Daman Duwalia."

"What would Daman have been doing in Bakersfield?" Pete asked excitedly.

The Three Investigators had met Daman Duwalia two summers before, in a case that involved the Rocky Beach Summer Theatre Festival where Daman had been starring with Pete's now-girlfriend Califia in a production of *Romeo and Juliet*.

His latest film in the *Time Twist* franchise had opened the previous July 4th, and Pete and all the others had been invited to the premiere and an after-party. Worthington, in his acting days, had been in a movie with him when Daman was still a boy. They'd sent him the e-mail about their new Headquarters but they hadn't heard from him.

"If it was him, then I presume he was line dancing," Worthington said.

How cool would that be! Pete thought. Maybe it really *had* been Daman Duwalia at the Roundup! In fact, as the six of them got ready to head back to Rocky Beach, Pete felt as if his heart was in this case for the first time ever – maybe because seeing Jupiter on the hunt for answers was always something that bucked Pete up.

However, as he looked out the window at the Central Valley, Pete had to admit that he'd been electrified to learn that Mateo's summer job was running a roller-coaster on which a cart had crashed to the ground once, killing one of its riders. Although Pete liked to think he'd put his superstitious past behind him, a haunted roller-coaster had been bound to grab his attention!

6

## A Plea To Daman Duwalia

The next day, Bob got to the Salvage Yard in the middle of the morning. They were going back to Bakersfield, just as Jupiter had told Mateo. But because the day before had been so long and tiring, they'd decided not to start too early. After they'd dropped Wally off at Isabella's, they'd gone back to the Salvage Yard to do some basic planning, and after that, Bob had gone home and given his father the Writer's Dice that Pete's mother had wrapped in silver paper. The dice had been a big success, and he and his father had stayed up late learning how to use them. They'd laughed a lot.

Now, Bob parked his bike in the shade of the outdoor workshop and took off his backpack. It was heavier than usual since it contained the clothes and other belongings he'd need for a couple of nights away from home.

After what had happened on their first trip, everyone had been enthusiastic about returning, and Bob had been very relieved to learn that. Up until the time they'd walked through the orange grove and seen the dead trees, he'd remained apprehensive about having told Mrs. Crenshaw they'd look into it for her sister. But by the time they'd left the amusement park, he'd felt pleased that he had done so. As he walked into HQ2 through the double doors leading to the outside workshop, he found he was the last to arrive.

Mallory was sitting in a butterfly chair hunched over her laptop, Pete was sprawled in a beanbag chair, and Jupiter was pacing, his hands behind his back. All three of them had piled their backpacks by the double door, and Bob dropped his with the others.

"What are you doing, Mallory?" he asked.

"Checking out cheap motels in Bakersfield," Mallory said.

Bob laughed. "So Jupe, did you have a revelation in the night about the goat shed?"

"I did," Jupiter said, sitting down. "Saint Peter appeared to me and said, 'Stay in a motel.'"

"I thought you were so concerned about money," Bob said. Since the beginning of the summer, Jupiter had been worried that they would run out of funds before the end of August. The renovation of HQ2 had been more expensive than any of them had thought it'd be.

"I *am* worried about money," Jupiter said. "But I'm assuming that sometime in the next ten months we're going to get a finder's fee for the sale of the Ngil mask, and in the meantime, I think we'll be happier in a motel than on the floor of a goat shed."

"It might not have been that bad," Pete said. "I mean, we've slept on the floor before. Remember when we camped out in the attic of Connor O'Malley's house in Auburn?"

"Of course," Jupiter said. "But this is different. And anyway, I'm afraid there might be too much – well, *atmosphere* at the Golden Globe for us to get any real work done."

Bob understood. He thought that Jupiter was probably right. The Robertsons had seemed very intent on being good hosts when they'd gotten there yesterday, and in a case like this one, you needed a certain distance to get the right sort of mind-set to investigate.

"So did you find a cheap place to stay?" he asked Mallory.

"That's all there are in Bakersfield," Mallory said. "Other than the Bakersfield Marriott and the Padre Hotel. Most of the rest of the places to stay are motels, and they're a lot less expensive than the ones in Rocky Beach or Los Angeles. They look perfectly fine, and most of them have swimming pools. I guess it's just that not that many people go to Bakersfield for vacation."

"So did you pick one?" Bob asked. While he might have been imagining it, it seemed to him that, for just a second or two, Mallory looked embarrassed.

"Well, sort of. I mean, I'd heard of this place before. From someone who came to the Salvage Yard. A biker. He was heading north to go camping, but he was going to stop in Bakersfield, and he told me that if we wanted a place to stay up there, we should stay at The Oasis."

"The Oasis?" asked Bob. "Is that a resort?"

"Hardly," said Mallory. "It's the kind of old-fashioned motel where, instead of an inside corridor, the doors open to the outside where you park. I've never stayed in one like that, but they seem as if they'd be a lot of fun. I made reservations for a couple of nights. Two rooms next to each other with two double beds in each."

"Who was this biker, exactly?" asked Pete.

"Oh, just some guy looking for a part for his bike," said Mallory. "His nickname was Cueball."

"He plays pool, then?" Jupiter asked dryly.

"Actually," Mallory said, "he's just plain bald. I thought he was pretty interesting. A kind of American guy I've never really met before. He said he and three of his friends were going to some sort of bikers' convention later this summer in South Dakota. But for now, they're just heading for Idaho."

"Are they going to be at the motel when we get there?" asked Pete.

"I have no idea," Mallory said. "But The Oasis is right across from The Roundup and since we heard about that place both from Pete's uncle and from Worthington, I thought it would be a good location."

"We can take our own bikes," Pete said, " – the other kind – and get back and forth from the motel to my aunt and uncle's or to the carnival that way. Though it's a bit of a ride."

"Is Worthington taking us again?" Bob asked.

"He can't," Jupiter said. "He was already booked, but I asked my aunt and she said that Leif can take us up this afternoon.

He'll drive us in the Flex, so we can fasten our bikes to the back and there's plenty of room for our backpacks and other gear."

So they were all set, Bob thought. He was looking forward to it. He had no idea what sorts of things might happen, or what they might discover in a few days away, but in the past, whenever The Three Investigators had worked hard, they'd turned up interesting and unexpected information – and he sensed that by this time he and Jupiter and Mallory all wanted to do everything they could to help Pete's family.

"Anyway," Pete said. "Listen to this! Remember when Jupe asked my aunt to send us stuff about who'd bought the supplement and who the monthly subscription customers were? Gabriella just sent through the lists. Guess who gets oranges every month from the Golden Globe! Daman Duwalia!"

"Daman?" Bob said, "Really? Then it really *was* Daman that the waitress saw at the Roundup!"

"Isn't it a hoot what a small world it is?" Pete said. "I mean, everyone loves navel oranges, and as Uncle Dave said, his are the best in the world. But it still knocks me out that Daman orders from them."

"Do we have any idea how it happened?" Bob asked. "Was Daman shooting a movie in Bakersfield?"

"When we found his name," Pete said, "we were so curious that I called my aunt − I had to call her anyway to say that we were coming back − and I asked how it had happened."

Bob could see how excited Pete was by the coincidence. The fact that Pete's family supplied Daman with oranges doubled down on the connections between Pete and Daman.

"She told me that Daman had been staying at some resort in the southern Sierras and he'd been passing through Bakersfield, right by the Golden Globe," Pete said. "Don't you remember him telling us about some place he likes to go to in the mountains? Anyway, he'd driven in on a whim and had eaten an orange right there, outside, in front of the stand, and he'd liked it so much that he ordered them to be delivered every month they were in season!"

"Of course," Jupiter said, "just because Pete's aunt and uncle send him oranges doesn't mean he hangs around Bakersfield. But I do think that if we tell him the Robertsons are in trouble, he might be willing to help us, if we need it. Remember how Per Jorgensen helped us last summer when we were interviewing Ivan's high school classmates? They were much more ready to cooperate when a famous actor was involved. Maybe Daman would be willing to make a phone call or two if we needed help. Even bureaucrats aren't immune to the lure of celebrity. A call from Daman Duwalia saying we were friends of his or something might open some doors."

"I'm sure he'd help," Pete said. "He's helped us every time before. Remember when we asked him to forward our Twitter message about the kidnapper's car when Adam got grabbed? He did it right away, to his gazillion followers."

"There weren't *that* many," Jupiter said. "But there *were* a lot."

"So when do we leave?" Bob asked.

"Leif said he'd be ready to leave at about 12:30, right after lunch," Jupiter said. "So that gives us a couple of hours to do some research and to try to get our thoughts in order."

"What did you have in mind, Jupe?" Bob asked as he got out his laptop and settled down in one of the butterfly chairs. All four of them were now close to one another in the hang-out area.

"I thought we ought to check out this Rapid Response Commission," Jupiter said. "After all, they're the ones who have closed down the Robertsons' shop."

Bob typed "California Rapid Response Health and Safety Commission" into the search bar. Soon he was on the commission's site. Across the top was a sky-blue banner on one side of which the cast-iron dome of the California State Capitol in Sacramento appeared, rising above its stark white supporting columns. The site was text- and graphics-heavy, with lots of links, and a menu bar down the right-hand side. Bob saw a link for Public Comments and clicked on it. He was taken to a page where ordinary citizens had posted remarks about their experiences with the Commission. Bob laughed.

"Listen to this!" he said. "They have a place for people to write in. This is from L.T. in Truckee. 'Another utter waste of taxpayer money. Stop protecting me from stuff I don't need protection from.'"

"Wow!" Mallory said. "Not exactly a vote of confidence. Are all the comments like that?"

Bob shook his head. "No," he said. "Here's one from P.M. in Vallejo. 'Thanks for coming so quickly. You saved my bees.'"

"What does that mean?" Pete asked.

"Who knows?" Bob said. "But from what I can see there are a lot of complaints. Most people seem to find the commission intrusive, dumb, and unnecessary."

"Is it centralized in Sacramento?" Jupiter asked.

"My dad said every county has its own team," Pete said.

"Bob," Jupiter asked. "See if there's a listing of the teams by county."

Bob went back to the Home Page and found a list of live links. He clicked on Kern County. The county seat was Bakersfield, and there was a picture of the four people who worked in the Rapid Response Team office there, on Q Street. Arsenio Santiago smiled widely, together with two other men and a woman. It surprised him that the team was so small. Kern County was pretty big.

"Here's a picture of Santiago," Bob said. "It looks like he's the main guy. His bio says that he was born in Bakersfield and went to school there, including the state university. He's worked for the government ever since graduation, one agency after another."

"A dyed-in-the-wool bureaucrat," Jupiter

said.

"It says here that now he wants to dedicate his life to the health and safety of his fellow citizens."

Pete blew a raspberry.

Mallory laughed. "All officials say stuff like that. What is he supposed to say? 'I got this job, and all I care about is my salary and my pension'?"

"That's true," Pete said. "But still."

Mallory went on. "But we still don't understand why Santiago shut down the Robertsons. It's possible that there's been a simple error somewhere in the supply chain and that the supplement somehow got polluted by mistake. If there were consumer complaints, then this commission was certainly within its rights to check out the supplement. But it's also possible that someone for some reason is going after Robertsons' Remedies on purpose."

"But why would anyone do that?" Pete asked. "My aunt and uncle have never hurt anybody."

"We have no idea," Jupiter said. "That's why trying to discover motives is so important in what we do. If we could find a motive, we'd have a suspect. But of course, as Mallory said, this might have just happened innocently, with nobody behind it. It's the fact that the trees were also poisoned that's making us so suspicious."

"But why didn't Santiago just tell my aunt and uncle to stop selling the one supplement if that's where the problem was?" Pete asked. "Why shut down the whole operation? They sell lots of other things besides the San Joaquin Valley supplement – not to mention all the fruit."

"That's a very good question, Second," Jupiter said. "And it bears looking into. Of course, it was easier for him to shut the whole operation down than to take one product off the market. And customers might have been worried that if there were problems with one product, there might be problems with all of them."

"We have to remember that Santiago was pretty nice, all things considered," Bob said. "And Mateo said he was semi-decent."

"Still," Jupiter said. "We can't rule out good old-fashioned corruption."

"What do you mean?" Pete asked. "You think someone is paying Santiago to hurt my aunt and uncle?"

"Always a possibility," Jupiter said. "Still, as I said before, we need to find a motive for *someone* before we can go around suspecting that Santiago's interference is anything other than incompetence or a simple mistake."

"Did Gabriella send through sales records of the supplement along with the monthly fruit customers?" Bob asked. There was no reason to look at the list of people who got fruit each month. Mallory, Jupiter, and Pete had already studied it, and all they'd come up with was Daman Duwalia. But maybe the other list would give them some information.

Jupiter handed Bob the PDF that they'd printed earlier.

He scanned it quickly. It was quite extensive; Mrs. Robertson surely had been right when she said it was their best seller.

The sales records were divided into mail order sales and shop sales for the past six months. "Why don't I look at the shop sales?" Bob said. "Pete, why don't you and Mallory look at the mail order sales?"

As Bob looked down the shop sales, he came across the ten bottles that Franklin Weaver had purchased. It had been the first Wednesday in February, almost five months ago.

"It's no wonder Gabriella remembered the sale to Mr. Weaver so vividly," he said. "It had never happened before. Or since. Two bottles is the most anyone else ever bought. At least in person."

"Nevertheless," Jupiter said. "While I was suspicious of such a large purchase earlier, my suspicions went away after we talked to Billy Taylor. It makes perfect sense to me that someone who got Valley fever as a kid would be anxious about it. Are there any large online orders?"

"Definitely!" Pete said. "Here's an order for twenty bottles. And another one for twenty-five! Much more than for any other supplement. That must mean it's really excellent!"

"Are people buying it in bulk and then reselling it?" Bob asked. "At a markup?"

"That could be possible," Mallory said. "After all, the Robertsons do offer a discount depending on the size of the order."

"Anything else you want us to research, Jupe?" Bob asked. He knew from experience that Jupiter would track down all the angles and try to find out as much about each of them as he could.

"Yes," Jupiter said. "Check out Franklin Weaver. Even though he may have had an excellent reason for buying a lot of Mateo's supplement, I found the process by which Mateo was hired for the amusement park a little odd. It's one thing for Franklin Weaver to have been impressed with Mateo when he stopped by the Robertsons' grove, and another thing entirely to have offered him $2000 as a bonus at the end of the summer season if there were no accidents or problems with The Nemesis. Why would he think there even might be? He may make a lot of money pretending the ride is haunted, but he himself must know perfectly well that it isn't."

"That's true," said Pete. "I hope he really pays up!"

Bob found a lot of information almost immediately – solid feature pieces about the Citrus and Carnival Ranch and how great it was for the area children, stories about buildings in downtown Bakersfield that Weaver had bought and renovated and was now renting, a long article when Weaver had been honored by the local Kiwanis. There were multiple pictures of him. Jupiter stared at several of them thoughtfully.

"He looks all right," Bob said.

"Well, he doesn't have a handlebar mustache and small glinty eyes," Jupiter said, "if that's what you mean. But as we've discovered again and again in our investigations, people are not always as they seem." He thought for a moment. "See what you can find out about Valley fever," he said to Bob.

Bob found a number of articles, some in medical journals. Its medical name was coccidioidomycosis and it was caused, as they knew, by two fungi in the soil. When the soil was churned up and became airborne, people could breathe them in.

"It settles in the lungs," Bob said, "and it causes fever, coughing, and tiredness."

"Does Western medicine have a cure?" Jupiter asked.

"Not really," Bob said. "Most mild cases get better on their own. Get plenty of rest, drink lots of fluids, that sort of thing. But more severe cases are treated with anti-fungal drugs."

He clicked on another link. "Wait a minute," he said. "Here's a reference to a product that's being tested as a potential cure."

"The company?" Jupiter asked.

"It's called Tehachapi Biogen. And listen to this! It's on 20th Street in downtown Bakersfield! It looks like it's a biotech startup," Bob said.

"Excellent work, Records," Jupiter said. He was pacing more quickly. "A biotech startup in Bakersfield is developing a product that would obviously compete in the same consumer market as the Robertsons' supplement."

"Unless it's going to be a prescription medicine," Mallory said.

"Does it say, Bob?" Jupiter asked.

"From what I can tell, it's just going to be an over-the-counter product," Bob said.

"Just like the San Joaquin Valley supplement," Jupiter said. "So it stands to reason that the people developing this new product have a motive for trying to damage the reputation of Robertsons' Remedies. Maybe there's someone – or a bunch of someones – at Tehachapi Biotech who consider the Robertsons professional competitors."

"Wow!" Pete said. "I see what you mean about how finding a motive can lead to finding a suspect."

"Can you uncover more about this Tehachapi place?" Jupiter asked.

Bob Googled the company's name and found its website. The home page featured a picture of the reception area on 20th Street as well as a lab. Under fluorescent lights, people wearing oversized white coats, white masks, and goggles hovered over microscopes.

Bob also found a roster of the people

who worked for the startup. The Head of Research was a man in his early forties named Dr. Ishaan Chakrabati, and his staff of six included two other biochemical engineers named Rahul Banerjee and Advik Chopra.

Chakrabati had been born in India and had come to the United States to study biochemical engineering at UCLA. He was now a naturalized citizen. He spoke both English and Hindi.

"Wait a minute," he said. "Doesn't Daman Duwalia speak Hindi?"

"Yes," Jupiter said. "I believe he does."

"Here's an idea," Bob said. "It turns out that the head of research at this company is from India and speaks Hindi. Maybe we could ask Daman to pose as a private investor. Between his fame and the fact that he speaks Hindi, I bet he could cut through a lot of smoke very quickly."

"That's brilliant, Records," Jupiter said. Bob could see, both from Jupiter's expression and from his tone of voice, that he was really impressed.

"We could ask him just to make a phone call," Pete said.

"I don't know," said Bob. "A meeting in person might have a bigger impact. It probably wouldn't take him more than an hour or so. Once he got to Bakersfield, I'm sure, given who he is, they'd meet with him whenever he wanted to."

"Why don't you write Daman an e-mail?" Jupiter suggested, "asking him if he'd be willing to help us. Be sure to mention that it's Pete's family who's in trouble."

Bob took his laptop to the back of the building, to the place they were calling their office. He set himself up and quickly wrote the letter. It came easily – after all, it had been his idea, and when it had come to him, he'd already imagined asking Daman. He made sure to include his cell phone number, checked the letter for typos, and triumphantly hit SEND.

## 7

## A Glimpse of Franklin Weaver

Jupiter glanced at his watch. It was just after 2:00 in the afternoon as the Flex, with Leif Haldorrson driving, climbed the steep grade that would take them over Tejon Pass on Interstate 5. Tejon Pass connected coastal southern California and the Central Valley, of which the San Joaquin Valley was the southernmost section. Once they crested the pass over the Tehachapi Mountains, they had another fifty minutes to go before they reached Bakersfield.

Jupiter had been over the pass just yesterday – not to mention the many times he and the other Three Investigators had driven north for one case or another. Still, he'd never gotten used to the descent. It was a dizzying drop of over 2600 feet in a little over eleven miles. It twisted and turned and half of it was precipitously steep. There were two ramps for runaway trucks. He felt a bit queasy. Of course, he had always had an odd fear of heights. Luckily, it hadn't interfered much with his work as an investigator.

He closed his eyes tightly and tried to focus on the case. It had a lot of threads to it, but so far the most interesting facts he had encountered were about Franklin Weaver. Of course, he also had questions about Arsenio Santiago and why he had shown up at the Golden Globe Citrus Grove yesterday.

Still, what had really snagged his mind was the way he kept going back and forth on thinking that Franklin Weaver might be behind some of the things that had been going on. He'd been quite sincere telling the others that when he'd first heard that Franklin Weaver had bought ten bottles of the San Joaquin Valley supplement, he'd been a bit suspicious. But when he'd learned from Billy Taylor that Weaver had had Valley fever as a child, he'd decided the man had a good reason to want to never catch the disease again.

However, although Franklin Weaver might have been impressed enough by Mateo when he met him to want to hire him for the summer, it was strange, to put it mildly, that he had offered to pay him a $2000 bonus if nothing went wrong on The Nemesis. This whole business with a haunted roller-coaster seemed a little dodgy.

And while it was true that Mateo actually *did* live right next door to the amusement park and might be helpful if the park needed a pinch hitter, still, the fact of the matter was, Franklin Weaver had tried to buy the Robertsons' citrus grove five years before, and when he hadn't been able to, he had developed an amusement park and you-pick-it business which had taken a lot of commerce away from the Robertsons. Also, his place really *was* in an ideal location for him to send in someone to poison the Robertsons' trees. For all of these reasons, you really could make a pretty solid argument that Franklin Weaver couldn't be seen as the Robertsons' friend, Jupiter thought.

As for Arsenio Santiago, Jupiter, Mallory, Pete, and Bob needed to know a lot more before they could decide whether there really *was* a problem with the supplement, or whether Santiago was either incompetent or corrupt. If someone from Tehachapi Biogen had used Arsenio Santiago to shut down Robertsons' Remedies, then he or she also had to have had the opportunity to infiltrate the Rapid Response Commission.

Jupiter could tell from the difference in the sound of the motor that they'd made it safely to the bottom. He opened his eyes warily and was delighted to see the flatness of the San Joaquin Valley stretching in front of him. Whoever had thought the flatness was boring had never been over Tejon Pass. Mallory, too, had opened her eyes. Jupiter took a deep breath and stared out the window.

Not long past Grapevine, Interstate 5 turned north up the Central Valley, and Leif stayed straight on State Highway 99. Forty minutes later, as they reached the outskirts of Bakersfield, Jupiter was still thinking about the possibility that someone at Tehachapi Biogen had used Arsenio Santiago to try to shut down Robertsons' Remedies. He wondered if he ought to ask Leif to take them on a short side trip to 20th Street.

"We're here!" Pete said. "Plenty of time to unpack and take a swim before dinner."

"So much time, in fact," Jupiter said, "that it might be wise if we stopped at the offices of Tehachapi Biogen. We can try to get a feel for the place in case Daman gets back to Bob about it. What do you think?"

"I think it's a good idea," Bob said.

Mallory agreed. "There'll still be time for a swim, afterwards."

"It's on 20th Street, downtown, Leif," Jupiter said. "I hope you don't mind. We won't be long."

"That's fine," Leif said. "Just tell me how

to get there."

"I'll check my phone," Bob said, pulling it out of his pocket. He tapped the screen, then studied it for a moment. "Just stay straight on 99 until you get to 58 East. Then you turn right."

Jupiter found the area to the southwest of Bakersfield pretty depressing. The sun beat down on small shabby ranch houses surrounded by chain link fences and blasted yards, rows of single story apartment buildings, and dispiriting strip malls with Subways, auto parts stores, massage parlors, and boarded up businesses. As they turned onto 58 East, Jupiter could see that the city was mostly urban sprawl, almost all of the buildings low and squat, with just a few taller structures that seemed to mark the downtown.

As they turned north on Route 204, Jupiter began seeing evidence of urban renewal. Recently renovated buildings stood near ones that were being torn down or refurbished. They passed a Chinese and a Vietnamese and a German restaurant, signs for the high school and elementary school, various taquerías and independent grocers with gleaming glass storefronts. They took a left on Thruxton Avenue. Jupiter caught a glimpse of the newish Amtrak station with its glass walls and red sandstone base and a little later they passed the Mechanics Bank Arena with its plaza and fountain, quite flashy.

The train station made Jupiter think of Billy Taylor and his story about playing chicken with the trains when he was in high school. This was the passenger terminal; he didn't know where the railyards were, where the boxcars arrived and took off with their loads of produce. Maybe they were up in Oildale where Billy had grown up. That would make sense. There would also be tanker cars to take the oil away.

The city suddenly looked prosperous. People were walking on the sidewalks, and the shops and businesses seemed contemporary and stylish. Following Bob's instructions, Leif took a right onto M Street and then a left onto 20th. Five blocks later, across from Blue Oak Coffee and just down the block from the famous Fox Theater, they found the building that housed Tehachapi Biogen. It was quite upscale. Leif parked right in front.

The building was brick, steel, and glass. Jupiter peered through the tall windows at a lobby with potted trees and staircases to the upper floors. From a sign on the outside, Jupiter saw that Tehachapi was on the second floor, not far from a suite holding the offices of Dr. Jeffrey Finklestein, DDS.

"Pete, you and Bob should stay in the car with Leif," Jupiter suggested. "Mallory and I can pretend that our parents have sent us to see if the dentist is taking new patients."

"Why do you want to do that?" Pete asked.

"It may be unnecessary," Jupiter said, "but it does seem like two teenagers walking into a biotech company with questions might raise suspicions."

"Well, O.K.," Pete said, "but I don't think you and Mallory look much like brother and sister."

Mallory laughed, at which Jupiter felt a bit embarrassed.

"What I meant," he said, "is that I'll pretend to be looking for a new dentist. Mallory can just be my friend."

"That'll work," Pete said.

The building was air-conditioned, and the air was blessedly cool. As they walked up the staircase, Mallory asked, "How do want to handle this?"

Jupiter shook his head. "I don't really know," he said. "We'll have to play it by ear."

When they reached the second floor, there it was – right in front of them, well before the dentist's offices. "Let's just go on in," Mallory said. There was an open reception office with several cubbyholes where people were working, and a back section closed off behind a white wall with two doors. Presumably the lab itself was back there.

Mallory seemed perfectly natural and at ease to Jupiter. She smiled encouragingly at him and then walked up to the reception desk where she was met by a very pretty Indian woman with a nose stud and long black hair pulled back in a ponytail. She looked like she was in her early 20s and wore a name tag that read Davshi Anand. There was a pile of brochures on the counter. Jupiter picked one up.

"Hello," the young woman said. "May I help you?"

"Hi," Mallory said. "We were just interested in what you do."

"Oh?" the woman said. "You saw that we're a biotechnology company? We use biological processes, usually on the cellular or molecular level, to develop products to make our lives better." She smiled at them. "I see your friend has already taken one, but here's a brochure for you as well. It will answer lots of your questions." She handed a brochure to Mallory.

She had a pleasant lilting voice that seemed to rise at the end of every one of her sentences, as if she were asking a series of questions. She seemed utterly incurious as to why two almost-sixteen-year-olds would be dropping by Tehachapi Biogen.

Next to the brochures was a stack of pamphlets.

"What are those?" Jupiter asked.

"Those?" Davshi Anand said. "Those are prospectuses. They lay out the financials of the company. They were put together with investors in mind, showing how investing money in the company would pay off. Are either of you rich?" She laughed gaily.

Jupiter opened the prospectus and looked down a long list of figures. "No," he said. "Not at the moment. But I know someone who might be interested. Would it be possible to get a list of your investors?"

Davshi shook her head. "I'm sorry. That information is confidential. I'm sure you can understand why."

Yes, Jupiter supposed he could. There was one kind of publicity the rich liked and other kinds they would rather avoid.

"But you do have to tell the government," he said.

"The government?" Davshi said. She laughed. "Of course, we tell the government. At tax time. Are you with the government?"

"Not today," Jupiter said.

"Well, if your friend is really interested," Davshi said, "we're having a public information session tomorrow, for new investors. Better tell him – or her! – to get in now, while the getting's good!"

Just as she said this, a man entered the reception area from the corridor.

"Good afternoon, Mr. Weaver," Davshi said.

"Good afternoon, Miss Anand," the man said.

Jupiter looked at him closely. It was indeed Franklin Weaver III. Jupiter recognized him from the photographs he'd seen earlier, back in Rocky Beach. He looked like a distinguished older businessman, if a bit overstuffed, rather than the owner of a carnival and orange grove. He was in his early seventies, Jupiter thought – the same age as Billy Taylor – dressed in a double-breasted pinstripe suit with shoes so highly polished they seemed to scatter light. He had a florid face with a shock of white receding hair, and he radiated an air of self-importance. He huffed a little and cleared his throat. "Is Ishaan here?" he asked.

"I'm sorry, Mr. Weaver," Davshi said. "Dr. Chakrabati is out for the rest of the afternoon. Do you want to leave a message?"

Weaver shook his head firmly. "No, no, that's fine." He gathered himself as if suddenly remembering who he was. "I heard you mention the investor's meeting as I was walking in," he said. He made his voice very jolly, though it sounded hollow to Jupiter. "It's for new investors, yes? No need for me to come, then, though of course I do have a certain interest in it." He paused. "Since I own the building where it's going to take place." He laughed as though this were a very good joke.

Davshi rushed to flatter him. "As well as the five buildings on either side."

Weaver smiled in a self-satisfied fashion. "Well, I'd better be going. I have business elsewhere. As always, it seems!" He nodded pleasantly to Jupiter and Mallory, swiveled on a heel and toe, and left.

"Thank you very much," Jupiter said to Davshi. "We should be going too. I'll talk to my friend. Maybe he can come to that meeting tomorrow. What time is it?"

"One o'clock," Davshi said.

"Thanks again," Mallory said, as the two of them left.

On the way down the stairs she said, "From what he said to the receptionist, it's hard to know whether Franklin Weaver is an investor in the company or just owns the building the company is in."

"I agree," Jupiter said. "And we should try to avoid leaping to conclusions about it. The fact is, I'm actually impressed – so far at least – with what Weaver has been doing with the buildings. Downtown Bakersfield is looking pretty good, and I don't think it would be if it weren't for him. He may have actually bought the land next to the Robertsons to develop it into an amusement park for the local kids, and not for anything more nefarious – or connected to the Robertsons."

The Oasis Motel was on the eastern side of Bakersfield – closer to Pete's aunt and uncle's property – and as they drove away from downtown, the upscale air dissipated; the streets seemed dispirited and a bit bedraggled.

Jupiter was pleased as they pulled into the motel's parking lot to find that Mallory had been right. The Roundup Bar and Bar-B-Q – the country-western place they'd heard about yesterday – was located just across the street.

While Jupiter couldn't have explained, if anyone had asked, just why he felt that it would be important to pay it a visit sometime, it was clearly a major local gathering place, and in a working class city like Bakersfield, places like that could be quite important sources of information. It had a façade of weathered wood and a number of hitching posts with wagon wheels leaning against them and a couple of cow skulls nailed to the walls. Neon signs flashed. The faint sound of honky-tonk drifted out into the large parking lot, which even now, at 4:00 in the afternoon, was filling up. The Roundup certainly was popular.

The Oasis was an old-fashioned motel that probably had been built in the 1950s, Jupiter thought. The swimming pool was smack dab in the middle of the asphalt parking lot. The room doors all opened to the outside. It was certainly more convenient than having to go down a long interior corridor, but it also felt as though the rooms were a bit more exposed to the world.

The woman at the desk was smoking a cigarette, and her hair was up in curlers. She had their reservations ready, and she gave them each a key to the rooms they'd share — Jupiter and Pete, Mallory and Bob.

Their rooms were on the ground floor, right next to one another as they'd requested. The motel had a second floor as well, with exterior stairways leading up to a balcony onto which the rooms opened. The balcony projected over the first floor rooms and was held up by wooden posts.

Most people, of course, would pull their cars right into the space in front of their room, but when Leif left, they'd have no car. Jupiter thought it might feel a bit peculiar to chain their bikes to the balcony's posts. Since it didn't feel like the safest neighborhood, perhaps they ought to bring them inside with them at night.

Each of the rooms had two double beds, a desk, a closet, and a bathroom. They were clean but had a strange smell – Jupiter didn't know if it was cleaning products or something else. The bedspreads were orange polyester and the carpets were dark and threadbare. It would only be for a few nights. Pete threw himself onto the nearest bed and bounced. "Not bad," he said.

They unloaded their gear from the Flex, unfastened their bikes from the racks, and then said goodbye to Leif, after thanking him for taking the afternoon to drive them. Jupiter made short work of unpacking. Then he stood in the room's open doorway, staring across at the Roundup. They'd been invited to the Robertsons' for dinner and the evening.

It was unbelievably hot. The flatness of the Valley seemed to concentrate the heat, and the concrete and asphalt of the urban center absorbed and reflected it.

"We still have time," Pete said. "Let's take that swim."

Jupiter and the others were easily convinced. They changed into their suits and trooped out to the pool. Pete jumped in, doing a cannonball, and yelled in delight. "The water's cool!" he said. Jupiter was glad of that. All he needed was to get parboiled in a swimming pool.

"I'm sitting this out," Bob said. He waved his phone. "In case Daman calls. I don't want to miss it."

Jupiter eased himself into the highly chlorinated water and began to swim laps. The third time down the length of the pool he could feel his body begin to unwind, to relax into doing something repetitive and rhythmic. He stopped thinking and concentrated on the stretch of his arms, the kick of his legs, and the sideways tilt of his head as he breathed. Pete and Mallory were laughing and splashing at one end of the pool; Bob sat hunched under an umbrella; and Jupiter swam and swam until he felt satisfyingly tired.

As he got out of the pool, his muscles tingled and water streamed from his hair. He stood there, toweling off and looking around him. He glanced across at The Roundup and was startled to see a man he was almost certain was Arsenio Santiago walking across the parking lot, hand in hand with a woman. He was dressed in jeans, a western-style pearl-button shirt, and cowboy boots.

Jupiter was surprised. Santiago had said he went to The Roundup just about every day, and it seemed he'd been telling the truth. He really was a regular – and maybe they'd be able to spy on him, Jupiter thought. Not for the first time, he wished that California wasn't a state in which the legal age for entering a bar was 21. Still, they could go to the barbecue, and if they ordered something to eat, they could probably wander into the bar and check out Santiago.

Maybe tomorrow night they could do that. The plan for the investigation was beginning to take shape. He put on his shirt and went to sit next to Bob. Mallory was now swimming laps, and Pete was horsing around with some kids who'd shown up at the pool with their parents.

As Jupiter sat there, in a pleasant haze, Bob's phone rang. Bob flashed a big smile at Jupe. "Here's hoping," he said. He flipped the phone open. "Hello," he said. "Bob Andrews speaking."

Jupiter hunched forward listening closely.

"Daman!" he said. "I guess you got my message." He listened carefully and his smile got wider. He gave Jupiter a thumbs up. He covered the receiver. "He'd love to help," he told Jupiter.

"That's great!" Bob said to Daman. "Thanks!"

Jupiter waved his hand at Bob. "Just a minute," Bob said. "Jupe wants to ask something." He covered the receiver again.

"When you wrote to him, we didn't know about the meeting tomorrow," Jupiter said. "But now we do, and I wonder – "

"Why don't you talk to him?" Bob said, handing the phone to Jupiter.

Jupiter cleared his throat. "Daman?" he said. "It's Jupiter. The thing is, since Bob wrote to you, Mallory and I did a preliminary reconnaissance at Tehachapi Biogen and we learned that they're having an open meeting for prospective investors tomorrow. Is there possibly a chance – ?”

“Hold on,” Daman said. There was silence for a while, and then he was back. “I checked on my GPS and it looks like I could get there from where I'm living in about an hour and a half. What time is the meeting?”

“One in the afternoon,” Jupiter said. “It's on 20th Street, right near the Fox Theater.”

“I'll be there,” Daman said. “But since I'm not an Investigator, it would be great if a couple of you came with me to the meeting. Not all four of you, though. That might look suspicious. Whoever comes, I can introduce you as fans who had won a prize to spend the day with me or something.”

To anyone other than Jupiter, this might have sounded a bit obnoxious, he reflected – but to him it simply sounded like a straightforward and intelligent way to dispose of a potential problem.

“That's an excellent idea,” Jupiter said. He had to make a quick executive decision – one based on very little analysis – and he ended up saying, “Mallory and Bob will probably meet you, then.

“That'll be great,” Daman said. “And

unless something comes up that I can't get out of in Los Angeles, I can see you and Pete afterwards. Maybe we can go out to the Golden Globe Citrus Grove and get caught up on things!"

As far as Jupiter could remember, it had been almost a year since they'd seen Daman. Two summers ago, when he'd contacted The Three Investigators to ask them to look into some trouble at the Rocky Beach Summer Theatre Festival, he'd just been a famous person who Pete had known about but who Jupiter hadn't.

Pete had been flattered and tickled that someone like Daman Duwalia was asking him and Jupiter and Bob to help him with a problem. And then he'd turned out to be just a regular guy – at least if a regular guy could also be described as a handsome seventeen-year-old Indian-American Brahmin who'd made it big in the movies but was nonetheless down to earth, capable of feeling frightened, and grateful for help.

"That would be excellent," said Jupiter. "Just so you know, we're staying at a motel called The Oasis."

"The Oasis?" asked Daman, sounding surprised. "I think that's right across from The

Roundup. It's a great country western bar. Even though I can tell that people sometimes recognize me, no one has ever bothered me. It's like stepping back in time to an older America. I'm actually in development on a movie inspired by Bakersfield and the Roundup."

"You are?" Jupiter asked curiously.

"I'll tell you about it tomorrow," Daman said.

"Great," said Jupiter. "Goodbye, then."

As he was hanging up the phone, Pete and Mallory, dripping water, joined him and Bob, and Jupiter quickly filled them in on what had just happened. Pete was very excited and Bob and Mallory seemed pleased as well.

"There's something else," he continued. "Right after I finished swimming, I was looking over at The Roundup, and I'm sure I saw Arsenio Santiago go in with some woman, probably his wife. It seems he's as much of a regular as he claimed to be. Maybe tomorrow night we can go check him out."

They went back to their rooms to shower and change for dinner, and then they were off. They rode their bikes through streets lined with small ranch houses. The neighborhoods were arid, with few trees or vegetation of any kind, and the streets were empty of kids riding bikes or playing ball. Soon they were in the country. Jupiter thought it was amazing how quickly they'd left the struggling city behind.

The roads were astonishingly flat and they made good time – though the trip took long enough so that by the time they got to the Golden Globe, Jupiter was starting to think that maybe the next day they should hire a taxi to take them wherever they needed to go in Bakersfield.

They had done that in San Francisco during their last case of the previous summer, and it had worked really well. In fact, Mallory was still in touch with the driver they'd met there – a woman named Andie McCorkindale. She'd been a very no-nonsense woman, quite well-educated and interesting, Jupiter thought.

Still, there was no need to make a decision tonight about how they would get around Bakersfield the following day. As Jupiter rode up the drive into the property, he was surprised to find the entire family in the final stages of putting together what looked to be an old road-side fruit stand. It had a slanted roof and a wide counter on which sat an old-fashioned cash register – brass with white buttons and embossed black numbers. Behind the counter there was room for the seller, and then raked shelves behind, to display the fruit.

"Uncle David!" Pete called as he got off his bike. "What's this?"

"Pete! Hi, everyone," Mr. Robertson said. "This old thing? We used to have it out on the main highway, before we renovated and set up our shop. It was sitting in the barn."

Mateo was on his knees, hammering. He drove the final nail and then stood up and shook Pete's hand. "I thought maybe if we put it together we could still sell our oranges and other fruit when people drove in. The shop may be closed, but there's no reason we can't sell everything but Robertsons' Remedies."

"They can't object to our selling the oranges," Mrs. Robertson said.

"Absolutely not," Jupiter said. "They can't."

"We didn't take down the CLOSED sign," Mateo said. "But we covered it over with a poster. It's got a picture of naval oranges hanging in a tree and our name – Golden Globe. Anyone who drives in won't know that the shop's been closed. They'll just think we've moved our operation outside for the summer."

Jupiter nodded. That all made eminent sense.

"And," Mateo continued, smiling slyly,

"somehow that yellow tape disappeared." He crossed his arms, looking quite satisfied.

Although this wasn't a permanent solution, Jupiter thought it would serve until he and the others came up with something better. The poster, with its glossy green leaves and large luminous oranges, was an example of the colorfully stylized illustrations of fruits and vegetables that Mallory had often sorted through in her job at the Salvage Yard – the kind that packers and shippers had long pasted to the wooden crates in which they sent their produce out into the market. Uncle Titus could never resist them on his buying trips.

It reminded Jupiter of the poster Mallory had given to Jupiter, Pete, and Bob as a memento of their third case the summer they met her. *That* had dated from 1888 and had advertised California itself rather than oranges or peaches or grapes. This was obviously much more recent. At the bottom of the poster, under the oranges, were big block letters that read GOLDEN GLOBE CITRUS, The Robertson Family.

It looked far better than the CLOSED sign it covered, but it still had a bit of age to it, and Jupiter thought that he should ask Pete's aunt and uncle if they – especially Mallory –

could take a look at all of the old stuff they had stored in their barns or sheds. You never knew what you might find in places like that – and they were just the kinds of places where Mallory's visual abilities could prove invaluable.

8

## Mallory Investigates

Mallory watched as Pete and Bob helped the family stack fruit in their new stand. Though she admired the family's resilience, it seemed totally incredible to her that the government of California would make them improvise like this just to keep earning money from the fruit they raised.

If the Health and Safety Commission really had found a problem with the Valley fever supplement, why had everything else the Robertsons sold gotten tangled up in the investigation? Why not simply tell them to stop offering that single product until everything was straightened out? It made no sense that the government would prohibit them from selling their soaps and salves and unguents – not to mention making it harder than necessary to sell their oranges.

These questions pressed upon her so urgently that, when she walked across to the others who were arranging oranges in neat pyramids, she asked them out loud.

"I wondered the same thing," Bob said.

"It seems like an excessive reaction."

"But don't government agencies always do whatever's easiest for them?" Mr. Robertson said.

"I guess," Mallory said. "My father was an engineer who specialized in bridges, and when he was designing and building them, he used to tell me how difficult it was to work with the government. He said he was always running up against stupid rules and regulations. Not ones that made the bridges safer – ones that made the bureaucrats safer."

Mr. Robertson laughed. "That's exactly what I meant," he said.

"I don't know why you're laughing," Mrs. Robertson said.

"How else can you respond to this?" Mr. Robertson said. "It can drive you crazy. It seems that most public policy is all about what the government sees as taking precautions. They pay no attention to anything that may happen in the future. All they care about is what might happen tomorrow. It's the definition of short-sighted."

"It sure is," said Pete. "But I really like that poster you've put on top of the Closed sign!"

"I do, too, said Jupiter. "Where did it

come from?"

"It was in the barn," Gabriella said. "When we went looking for the old roadside stand we found it, along with the cash register."

"It dates from my father's time," Mr. Robertson said. "He had it printed up soon after he bought the grove and renamed it. There's lots of stuff out there. In fact, when we renovated the store, we put everything we weren't using back there − those signed pictures of Merle Haggard and Buck Owens holding oranges I told you about, and other people my dad took pictures of."

"Maybe after dinner, the four of us can take a look at what you've got out there," said Jupiter. "It turns out that the motel where we're staying is right across the street from The Roundup Bar and Bar-B-Q where Mr. Owens and Mr. Haggard played once. Though that's not really my point. My point is that Mallory has a real talent for making sense of things like photographs and posters."

Mallory smiled when Jupiter said this, and she was glad when the Robertsons both agreed at once that, after dinner, someone would show her and the others the stuff that was stored away. When she and Jupiter had been checking out Tehachapi Biogen, she'd felt a little useless. Worse than that, although she was embarrassed to admit it, this case so far had been making her frustrated, and at the moment, the entire enterprise seemed to her downright claustrophobic.

For one thing, nice as Pete's aunt and uncle and cousins were, they were different enough from Pete and his mother and father that she hardly knew what to say to them. She liked thinking about things she had noticed – like the number and variety of American sub-cultures – and she *didn't* like sitting around trying to pretend nothing bad was happening when it obviously was.

Of course, ever since her father had died, she'd found it surprisingly hard to be around normal family groups, but in the case of Pete's aunt and uncle, there was something beyond that which made her feel awkward. Pete himself was interested in everything and was trying to learn all the time, but Mallory had the feeling that if he had started to tell his aunt and uncle about a paper he'd written the summer before – a paper about Stephen Decatur, one of the first naval heroes of what was then the brand-new United States of America – Mr. and Mrs. Robinson wouldn't have been all that interested in what he had to say.

The thing was, Decatur had been incredibly courageous after an American warship was captured by pirates in the Mediterranean, and Pete had taken heart from the story of the *Philadelphia* when he'd jumped through the skylight in the pottery studio to knock out David Wang and rescue Adam Suleiman during the last case of the summer before – and to Mallory, that was a great story, twice.

The truth of it was, she had a wild side to her nature – a wilder side than Jupiter, Pete, or Bob did – and while that was generally served quite nicely by being a Special Consultant to The Three Investigators, there was something about what Bob had called the nebulous nature of the Robertsons' problems that was starting to make her feel like screaming and running in the opposite direction.

She supposed she was also feeling a little disappointed that when she and the others had checked into the Oasis, she hadn't seen Robert Ackers – Cueball – and his friends there. She'd been hoping she would. Robert Ackers had made quite an impression on Mallory, largely because of what he had said about dumb bureaucrats and lying politicians. That he and his friends were big on being able to make their own decisions without any meddling – "If you'll pardon my language, Miss Mallory," he'd said.

Not only would she pardon it, Mallory thought sardonically, but she wished she was brave enough to use it herself on a day-to-day basis!

"Well," Mr. Robertson said. "Now that we've got this all ready for tomorrow, we might as well close it up. We're not going to have any more drive-in customers today. At least I hope not."

The shed had two barn-type doors on hinges. Once they were closed in the middle, the shed's contents were secure. Mallory helped the others clean up the wood scraps, nails, and tools left over from the reconstruction – after which they all went in to dinner. As they ate, Jupiter filled the Robertsons in on what they'd been thinking and doing, especially concerning Tehachapi Biogen.

Mr. Robertson was surprised to hear that the company had a product in development that might be in competition with the San Joaquin Valley supplement, and that Mallory and Jupiter had run into Franklin Weaver III. The Robertsons were especially surprised to hear that Daman Duwalia would be coming to

Bakersfield tomorrow to help them.

For some reason, this conversation, simple as it was, made Mallory even more itchy, and she was quite relieved when dinner was over and Mrs. Robertson suggested that Estevan and Gabriella show the Three Investigators the barn.

It was good to get outside. The barn was down a lane behind the house, just past the old goat shed. Part of it had been paneled with old pine, and as soon as they were inside, Mallory felt as if she was  on far more solid ground than she had been sitting in the Robertsons' house. The barn had a warm hazy feel to it, as if it existed in a time before electricity. It was dim, but there was still enough daylight streaming in the windows.

The Robertsons clearly used it as a storeroom, and it was filled with old things, some of them neatly arranged and ordered, some of them jumbled together – the kids' old bikes, a farmhouse sink, straight-backed wooden chairs in need of re-caning, old board games. There were picking ladders and canvas sacks the fruit pickers wore around their necks to keep their hands free, bushel baskets and spraying equipment and old irrigation hoses. There were household and decorative items, too – stacks of old ceramic bowls, cast-iron frying pans, a waffle maker, cut glass vases, milk glass plates.

Uncle Titus would have bought everything in the place and carted it back to the Salvage Yard. Mallory had worked there long enough by now that she'd gone through, organized, and inventoried all of the sheds and almost all of Uncle Titus's purchases. That wonderful sense of not knowing what she was going to find had pretty much vanished by now, but here it was again. There was nothing quite as great as going into an old storeroom packed with artifacts from the past.

As Mallory stood looking around her, Gabriella went over to a stack of boxes and started opening them. One of them had nothing in it but signed framed black and white photographs of people holding oranges.

Estevan handed them around and the four of them studied them. There was a photograph of a slim woman Mallory had never seen before, with long blond hair and heavy eye makeup. Her mouth was open and it looked as though she were about to take a bite of the unpeeled orange she held near her nose. She'd signed it "Love always, Nancy."

At last they came to the photographs of

Merle Haggard and Buck Owens. Haggard was trying hard to smile and wasn't quite making it. He looked uncomfortable holding an orange.

He wore a cowboy hat whose brim was bent down in the front. His forehead was furrowed with wrinkles, and he looked pretty old to Mallory. He wore a buckskin shirt and jeans, and above the wrist of the hand that held the orange Mallory could see what seemed to be a faded tattoo. The photo was signed "Yrs., Merle."

Buck Owens looked happier. He was smiling and seemed comfortable in his skin. His hair was sandy blond. In one hand he held a black cowboy hat with a hat band that looked like it was made of silver and turquoise, and in the other hand an orange. Because the photo was in black and white, the orange looked like it was the same color as the turquoise. The dark black of the hat jumped from the photo. It was signed, "Thanks! Buck."

"This is cool," Pete said.

Mallory agreed. It *was* cool – at least looked at in a certain way. However, since she very much doubted that either Buck Owens or Merle Haggard had anything to do with the troubles the Robertsons were experiencing,

Mallory looked around for something more substantial than photographs of famous people.

Just then, Pete pulled an old scrapbook from the box. It had a faded leather cover, and as Mallory looked over Pete's shoulder, he turned the pages. She saw that it contained clippings from the Kern County *Gazette* from the 1990s.

"Could I see that, Pete?" Mallory said.

"Sure," Pete said. He handed her the scrapbook and she sat cross-legged on the wooden floor and quickly scanned some of the clipped articles. She thought it must have been put together by Charles Robertson, Wally Tate's old friend. Almost all the articles mentioned the Golden Globe Citrus Grove.

But the headline that caught Mallory's eye read "Local Rancher Apprehends Teenage Vandals." It was dated March 1992. Mallory quickly calculated in her head – Charles Robertson must have been 67 then.

The article was full of quotes from Charlie, who was more than happy to tell his story. He'd been sleeping poorly and had been awakened by what sounded like laughter coming from the middle of his orange grove. He got out of bed quietly so as not to disturb his wife, and then he'd rousted two of his hired men who were sleeping in the barn.

He had a shotgun and the two other men carried shovels. They'd crept closer as the raucous laughter continued, and when they were close enough, they'd turned on their high-powered flashlights and shocked three teenage boys sprawled at the base of one of the trees. The ground around them was littered with empty beer cans, cigarette butts, and crushed oranges. The boys were slightly drunk and they said that they'd picked some oranges to eat and then had picked some more and started jumping on them – squashing them with their boots for fun.

Charles Robertson and the two men had collared them and marched them back to the house. Charles had called the police, and the boys had been arrested for property damage and littering and unlawful trespass. Their names had been withheld because they were juveniles.

Mallory found another article pasted near it. This one was titled "Vandals Sentenced to Community Service."

"Well, if we were looking for a motive," Mallory said, "we've found one." She quickly told the others the gist of the articles. "I bet the boys thought they were just horsing around, and that the punishment and public humiliation they got were out of proportion to what they did. Maybe it was. Those boys – well, they'd be men now – might have a motive for hating the Robertsons. A bigger motive than Franklin Weaver might have, and possibly even more than anyone at the tech company. We have to find out who these three boys were. Or are."

As Mallory said this, she felt her claustrophobia lessening. There was nothing like making some progress to put the heart back into a case.

Jupiter agreed. "Good detective work, Mallory," he said.

They were about to walk back to the house, the scrapbook under Mallory's arm, when Estevan pointed to an old wooden box in the corner. "You should take a look at that," he said, "if you like this other stuff."

The wood was weathered gray, somewhat split, and smeared with dirt, but as she walked over to it, Mallory could see the stenciled words "Central California Ice Company" and "Ice House, Sweet Briar Avenue, Lindsay, California."

Wow! she thought. That was the company Wally and Charlie Robertson had worked for when they were teenagers.

"Did you know your grandfather worked for this ice company when he was about your age?" she asked Estevan.

Estevan nodded. "My father told us all the stories. That's why it's so neat that we found it a couple of summers ago, buried under the barn floor."

"It was buried?" Jupiter asked.

"My dad was putting down a new wood floor," Estevan explained. "The old one was broken up and rotting, and the workmen were moving the dirt around, leveling it out, and they hit this old wooden box and dug it up. My dad said it must have belonged to his father when he was a kid. It was stuffed with old comic books and mystery stories and westerns. It's also got stuff he collected from school — sports stuff, trophies. Dad sold some of the comic books to a collector, but the rest of the stuff's still there."

Mallory took the lid off the ice company box. There were still a few comics left, their covers ripped and some of the pages missing, obviously not collector material, as well as some pulp fiction, its acid-soaked paper brittle and orange-yellow at the edges. There was a Boy Scout merit badge sash and a bunch of small inexpensive trophies, baseball players and football players standing on one foot on a square base with an engraved label. One of the baseball players was missing an arm. The gold coating was tarnished and flaking off. There were some ribbons, blue and red.

Mallory didn't quite know why she wanted to keep track of the box's contents, but she did. She pulled a notebook and pencil out of her pocket and carefully noted down everything.

*Captain Marvel. Adventure Comics. Superman. Death at Midnight. The Avengers.*

The engraving on the trophies was hard to read. Mallory rubbed them with her thumb. Valley League Champs 1938. MVP Lindsay Cardinals Baseball 1939. Runners-Up Valley League 1940.

"We better head back," Bob said. "We've got about a half-hour bike ride ahead of us and we want to get to the motel before dark."

"O.K.," Mallory said. "I'm all done here." She put the notebook in her pocket, and they returned to the farmhouse to say goodbye to the Robertsons. Jupiter assured them that they'd stay in touch and let them know about any developments in the case. Pete hugged his aunt and shook hands with his uncle and they were off.

The air was cooling down as they pulled out of the gravel drive and started back to the motel in the gathering twilight. As she rode, Mallory found that although she *was* glad to have found at least three people who might have a motive for wanting to hurt the Robertsons, she wasn't as glad as she'd thought she was when she first discovered the scrapbook.

After all, teenagers *did* grow up, and the person who had had them arrested had been David Robertsons' father, not David Robertson himself, and – oh, well, it had been  a long day, one way and another. She was looking forward to taking a shower and going to bed.

When they were close to the Oasis, she could hear the thump of country music from the Roundup. Oh, no, Mallory thought. While The Roundup had seemed appealing in the abstract, it hadn't occurred to her  before that it might be quite this *loud*.

But as she and the others turned their bikes into the parking lot of their motel, she was thrilled to see four Harley Davidson motorcycles standing in the parking spaces in front of two of the rooms, their silver and black bodies gleaming darkly under the parking lot's sodium lights – the curving dip of the seats, the large headlights, the hard plastic saddlebags on either side, the straight silver stretch of the exhaust pipes.

Not far away, four men were sitting on plastic chairs drinking beers. One of them seemed to be bald and wore a red bandana over his scalp. Three had long hair; two wore it stringy and loose, and one in a ponytail, and they all had beards. They were wearing bikers' leathers, punched with silver studs.

And although, under other conditions, Mallory might have given these men a wide berth, since one of them was almost certainly Cueball, she said to Pete, who was next to her, "I think that's the biker I told you guys about. The one who said we should stay at the Oasis. Let's go say hello."

With Pete, Bob, and Jupiter following – though seeming a little puzzled – Mallory led the way to where the bikers were sitting. She felt oddly excited to be taking the lead in such a peculiar situation, and when Robert Ackers stood up and said, "Is that Miss Mallory?", she also felt a rush of pleasure.

"It sure is," she said. "We took your advice, Cueball. If I can call you that."

The other three men laughed loudly. All four set their beers down on the pavement, then clambered to their feet. They wore bandanas – red and blue and green. One of them had taken part of his hair and braided it thinly. One of them wore an eye patch.

"Let me introduce everybody," Cueball said. "I'm Robert Ackers, and these are my friends John and George and Burt." Each of them nodded when his name was mentioned. "But as I already told you, our nicknames are what we really go by. John's is Buzz, George's is Knuckles, and Burt's is Rooster."

"Pleased to meet all of you," Mallory said. "I'm Mallory MacLeod, and these guys are Bob Andrews, Pete Crenshaw, and Jupiter Jones. Otherwise known as The Three Investigators. I'm their Special Consultant and we're up from Rocky Beach on a case."

Although this pretty much broke Jupiter's oft-cited rule to never reveal information you didn't really need to, letting Cueball and the other bikers know why she and her friends were in Bakersfield seemed pretty necessary to Mallory. Besides, it immediately led to something interesting, when Rooster said, "Investigators, huh? What kind of investigators, exactly?"

"We investigate anything," said Jupiter. "That's our motto, actually." He dug in his pocket for his wallet, removed a Three Investigators card, and handed it to Rooster, who studied it gravely, then handed it to Cueball, who did the same.

"Are you thinking what I'm thinking?" Rooster asked.

"Maybe," said Cueball.

"Whoa!" said Pete. "You guys need some investigators for something?"

# 9

## Some New Developments

Twenty minutes later, Pete was sitting in a squeaky plastic chair by the side of the pool, together with Mallory, Bob, Jupiter, and the four bikers. Underwater spots illumined their faces with shifting aquamarine light. Six or seven other people staying at the Oasis were clustered in small groups talking quietly. The evening was cooling off nicely.

By now, Pete had expected to be in bed, asleep. He felt a little dazed; it had been a long day. But one thing had led to another, and for a while now he'd been listening to the bikers talk about themselves. It seemed that Buzz had a wife and three children under the age of ten. He worked at a shipping warehouse outside of San Diego. Rooster had a teenage son. He was single and worked as a journeyman electrician, but he'd gotten his high school girlfriend pregnant, and though he loved the boy, he told Pete and the others he'd been much too young to have a kid. Knuckles was a confirmed bachelor. He'd gone to community college and worked in sales.

As for Cueball, he had two kids, one thirteen years old and one ten. He lived with his girlfriend and was between jobs at the moment. Right now, he was in the middle of telling the short-form version of his life story, which had begun simply enough but had taken a surprising and somewhat befuddling turn.

Cueball had grown up in Bakersfield but his parents had moved north long ago. His brother Dennis – Denny as Cueball called him – had stayed put and now had a business in the city. Speedy Gonzales Courier Service.

"Speedy Gonzales!" Pete said. "I saw one of his panel trucks yesterday. At this place called the Citrus and Carnival Ranch. A sort of amusement park outside of town. There's a restaurant there, and a guy delivered something to a waitress named Dotty."

"Dotty?" asked Cueball curiously. "What did she look like?"

"She had cat eye glasses, a mole on her chin, and a pencil stashed behind her ear," Pete said.

"That's Dotty!" Cueball said. "Her sister Kitty works at The Roundup and has a crush on old Rooster here."

Pete glanced at Rooster – who seemed a little embarrassed. "Well, anyway," Pete said, "the truck had 'Speedy Gonzales Courier Service – 'We Get Your Package There Yesterday!' on the side, with a cartoon mouse wearing a yellow sombrero, white shirt and trousers, and a red kerchief!"

"That's Denny's business," Cueball said. He bought it from a Hispanic guy, and since it was doing really well he didn't change it."

So that had all been clear enough. But what Cueball said next had confused Pete. It seemed that Denny – who had a wife and three kids – had  recently been approached by some California state agency and told that it had reason to suspect that someone had been fiddling with the packages it had been delivering in recent months.

Cueball couldn't remember the name of the agency, but he said it had demanded full access to the company's records so that it could check to see that everything was on the up and up. Denny's wife had told him they should hire a lawyer before he did anything like that, but Cueball's brother hadn't thought he could afford it. He'd been worried about screwing up his business and had ended up giving the password to the firm's relevant computer files to the state agent – after which it seemed the agent had started to blackmail him!

"That's not how Denny put it," said Cueball. "But that's what it seemed like to me. Have you guys ever investigated anything like this? The reason I'm asking is that when I first met Miss Mallory here, I said a couple of nasty things about bureaucrats and politicians, and she seemed to agree with me about them."

"Well," Mallory said, "as a matter of fact, some California agency is also going after Pete's aunt and uncle. They have a citrus grove just outside Bakersfield, and some Health and Safety agency has basically shut it down.

"A citrus grove?" said Cueball. "What in tarnation could a citrus grove have done to deserve *that*? By the way, I've been to that Citrus and Carnival Ranch you were talking about, Pete. My brother's kids go there all the time, and the last time I was up here, I went with them. Rooster went, too. It has a bitchin' water slide, and a couple of roller-coasters – including one that is supposed to be haunted!"

Pete had been trying to put that haunted roller-coaster out of his mind, but now it came roaring back, in full force.

"We heard that some guy died on it, up in Fresno," he said.

"That's right," said Cueball. "Some of those rides used to be damn dangerous sometimes. They aren't any more, though, I don't think. Still, old Franklin Weaver seems to be making a mint of money pretending that that one *is*."

"My cousin Mateo is the one who's running it this summer," Pete said. "My aunt and uncle's citrus grove is right next door."

At the same time, Jupiter asked "Do you know Franklin Weaver?"

Cueball looked from one to the other, then decided to answer Jupiter first.

"Old Franklin?" he said, chuckling. "When I was a hell-raiser, I had a lot of run-ins with the guy. But I wouldn't say I know him. Not exactly. Anyway, what are you doing to help your aunt and uncle out?" he asked Pete.

"We *haven't* been able to help them," Pete said glumly. "At least not yet. Though it's only been three days since we first started trying."

"Well, listen," said Cueball. "Remember the throttle slide for my carburetor, Miss Mallory? Tomorrow I'm going to get it fixed, but after I do that, me and the guys will be free to take you four anywhere you want to go. On our bikes, I mean. In a place like Bakersfield, bikes like yours really have their limits. If you can give a look-see into my brother's problems with Speedy Gonzales, we can drive you around."

Wow! thought Pete. How great would *that* be! Unfortunately, he had the feeling Jupiter wouldn't think so. When he and Mallory and Bob all looked in Jupiter's direction, he appeared doubtful. For a moment, he pinched his bottom lip, and then he said, "We should have time to meet with your brother tomorrow. And we appreciate the offer of the ride."

Jupiter pinched his lower lip some more. "Maybe we should meet after breakfast and discuss this," he said.

"Why don't we meet *at* breakfast?" Buzz said. "You won't get a better breakfast anywhere than at the Roundup. How about 9 o'clock?"

"We'll see you then," Jupiter said. After which everyone said good night and headed back to their rooms. Pete was so tired that he just peeled off his clothes, crawled between the covers, and fell asleep.

The next morning he woke early to the air conditioner's hum. The blackout drapes kept the room dark, but hints of the morning crept in around the edges. Jupiter was still asleep, snoring lightly in the other bed.

Pete lay on his back, yawning and stretching. The digital alarm on the bedside table said it was already almost 8:15 They only had forty-five minutes to get to The Roundup if they didn't want to be late. He jumped in the shower, and by the time he was out and toweling himself off, Jupiter was showing vague signs of consciousness. "Up and at 'em, Jupe," Pete said.

Jupiter groaned and turned over, but Pete knew he'd stick to their schedule and would soon drag himself up. He took his hacky sack and went out to the parking lot. The Harleys were still in place, but their owners were nowhere to be seen. Pete presumed they must already be across the street, where a white banner with red letters stretched across part of the Roundup's façade, announcing SERVING BREAKFAST 6:30 – 11:00.

He'd been tossing the hacky sack from foot to foot for some time when the doors to the two rooms opened, one soon after the other, and he was joined by the still-sleepy crew. Pete kicked the hacky sack high and caught it.

"All right!" he said. "Let's go!" He pointed at the banner.

Once across the street, Pete held the

door of The Roundup open for his friends. As he walked in, he was hit by the faint smell of spilled beer. They stood at the front of a large empty dance floor, pale pine planks polished by thousands of shuffling feet. To the right was the Bar-B-Q, with its white aproned waitresses and its plain pine tables, and to the left was the bar, a long polished strip of dark wood behind which was a wall of mirrors and glass shelves holding liquor bottles. The deserted bar and dance floor were crisscrossed by strings of little white Christmas tree lights. Only the restaurant was open.

"This is great," Pete said. "They've set it up so that we can go to the restaurant and even the dance floor."

Jupiter nodded, satisfied. "That should make our assignment tonight a good bit easier."

A sign that read PLEASE SEAT YOUR-SELF stood at the  entrance to the restaurant. The tables were filled with people drinking cof-fee and eating.

"There they are," Mallory said. To Jupi-ter, she said, "So what do you think? Are we going to take them up on their offer of trans-portation?"

"I don't know yet," said Jupiter. "But

since I don't have any better ideas about the
Robertson case at the moment, I think we can
at least spare the morning to check into Cueball's brother's problem." He turned to Pete.
"Since he has a local delivery service, it's possible he actually knows your aunt and uncle –
and that they use his service."

At breakfast, everyone seemed a bit sub-
dued, but it was nice to be eating. Pete ordered
the Rancher's Double X, which kept him busy
for quite a while. When Jupiter asked if they
could put off a decision about whether or not
to take the bikers up on their offer, they all said
sure.

Cueball gave Bob his cellphone number
and told him to call anytime. After breakfast he
and Rooster were heading to his old bike shop
and old mechanic, Skeet, but after that they'd
be  free most of the day – and they'd be in The
Roundup again in the evening, for line dancing
and country western music. He also gave Bob
the phone number and address of Speedy Gonzalez, and told Jupiter that Denny would be expecting them this morning.

They were all just getting ready to leave
when their waitress, a woman named Kitty –
who Pete thought actually did look  a little like
Dotty – stopped by one last time to give them

their bills.

She'd been flirting with Rooster the whole time she was serving their table, and now she said to him, "You know, Burt, Robert's brother has been delivering a lot of packages here recently, and I think I may be falling for him."

"Oh, don't do *that*, darlin,'" said Rooster. "You know you've already got my heart."

"Oh, you," she said, slapping him on the shoulder.

"What kind of stuff?" Cueball asked.

"What?" asked Kitty.

"You said Denny was delivering a lot of stuff. What kind of stuff?"

"Oh, I don't know," Kitty said. "Most of it seems to be from the same company. And it's usually redirected from another address. All I know is that the manager asked me to sign for it when it comes."

"Really?" Jupiter said. Pete swung his head to look at him.

Kitty nodded. "A local company, that's all I remember. Except that it's got Robert in the title somewhere. You know I can never see that word without thinking of you," she said to Cueball teasingly.

Jupiter cleared his throat in a way that alarmed Pete. He wasn't choking, was he? He glanced at him, questioningly. "Jupe, you O.K.?"

Jupiter nodded. He was sitting back in his chair, pinching his bottom lip.

"Do you boys want anything else?" Kitty asked the bikers.

"Just the check, sweetheart," Cueball said.

She slapped him on the shoulder again and slipped it under his plate. He glanced at it, took out his wallet, and handed her a twenty and a ten. "Keep the change," he said.

"Aren't you the sweetest thing," Kitty said.

The four bikers stood up, their chairs scraping on the wood floor. "You kids take care of yourselves now," Cueball said. "Don't do anything we wouldn't do."

"That gives you a lot of leeway," Rooster said, and he, Knuckles, and Buzz started laughing.

After Jupiter had paid for The Three Investigators' breakfast and left a tip of their own for Kitty, they headed back to the Oasis to get ready for the day. It was later than Pete had thought – almost 10:30 – and they were due to meet Daman Duwalia at 1:00. Even so, Jupiter took a little extra time to explain to Pete and the others his apparent choking fit.

When Kitty had said that the packages being delivered to The Roundup frequently had "Robert" in their title, even Pete had figured the chances were good that the packages had shipped from Robertsons' Remedies' packing facility in Fresno. However, it hadn't occurred to him that someone other than the people who had placed orders might be redirecting the Valley supplement.

"What?!" Pete said.

"Well, it's possible, at least," said Jupiter. "Most courier services have a way for you to get online and redirect your package to a different address if you aren't going to be there to take delivery yourself. What if someone managed to get their hands on Robertsons' customer list – maybe by hacking into the computer at the place that fulfills the orders, or maybe by having access to the courier's deliveries? He or she could log in and divert the deliveries to The Roundup. Not for long, but for long enough to open the bottles and put something in the supplement that would irritate the stomach."

"You mean and then they'd reseal the

bottles and have them delivered to the customers who'd ordered them?" Bob asked. "So you think the problem isn't at the Fresno plant?"

Jupiter nodded.

"But who would do a thing like that?" Pete asked, outraged.

"Someone trying to hurt your aunt and uncle," Jupiter said.

"How did you ever come up with that theory?" Bob asked.

"I think Wally's story about his traffic ticket must have been floating around in my mind somewhere – about how a ticket that was supposed to go to Utah wound up being sent to Vermont. It's easy enough for things to be delivered to the wrong place, or to be diverted from one place to another."

"How many people do you think are in on this?" Mallory asked.

"First," Jupiter said, "we don't even know if it's true. But if it is, there's no reason to think that the manager of The Roundup is doing anything other than being agreeable to one of his customers. I mean, he *might* know what's going on, but he also might not. And if there's an online way to divert the packages, then Denny – Cueball's brother – might have no idea what's been happening either."

"Boy," Pete said. "I think that buttermilk biscuit made you smarter than ever! If someone's putting something into the capsules, then people might really have been complaining about their stomachs and Arsenio Santiago might have just been doing his job!"

"That's what I've been thinking," said Jupiter. "But before we draw any further conclusions, we need to talk to Cueball's brother."

When they were all ready, Pete and the others buckled on their bicycle helmets and started pedaling. It was hot in the sun, but luckily it wasn't far to the headquarters of Speedy Gonzalez, a small warehouse that fronted a large parking lot. Three of the company's vans with the sombrero-wearing mouse on the side were parked in front. They found a bit of shade at the edge of the parking lot where they caught their breath and tried to dry off a little. When they'd returned to their normal colors, they went in.

The front of the warehouse, where the office and reception area were, was air conditioned and Pete was relieved to be enveloped in the cool air. A tall thin guy in his early thirties, with shaggy hair and big ears with a pencil behind one of them, came over to the customer counter. He was chewing gum, really smacking

186

it.

"Help you?" he asked. "Sending something?"

"No," Jupiter said. "We were hoping to talk to Dennis Ackers."

"Denny?" the man said. "He just stepped out. But he should be back soon. You can wait if you want." He pointed at a row of molded plastic chairs against the wall.

"Thank you," Jupiter said.

However, before they'd even had time to sit down, the door behind them opened and the little bell attached to it rang gaily. A man entered, wearing a white uniform with a red kerchief around his neck. His hair was sandy blond, cut short, but Pete could see in the eyes and the mouth his resemblance to Robert the biker.

"Are you Denny Ackers?" Jupiter asked.

"You got me," the man said. "What did I do?"

"We met your brother yesterday," Jupiter said. "He and his friends are staying next door to us at the Oasis Motel."

Denny Ackers did a double take.

"Are *you* the guys Cueball called me about?" he asked. They were clearly younger than he'd expected. "O.K., then," he added.

"Come on back." He flipped up part of the counter, walked through and held it for them, then let it fall with a loud bang. He led the way to his private office where Jupiter introduced Bob, Pete, Mallory, and himself, and then gave him a card.

As always, Pete grinned in anticipation, but Denny just looked from them to the card and then back again, his expression sober. They sat for a moment in awkward silence until Jupiter said, "Your brother told us you've been having trouble with a government agent, but he couldn't remember what agency the man was with. Does he work for the California Rapid Response Health and Safety Commission?"

Denny looked at him in amazement and said, "Yes, that's right. How did you know?"

"I merely guessed," said Jupiter. "But we're working on a case that involves a local family who owns a small business that was just shut down by the Health and Safety Commission. Pete is the nephew of Dave and Lilliana Robertson, the people who own the business – a small citrus grove. But they also run a soap and salve and supplement company. The Commission has launched an investigation into one of their products. And we have reason to believe that your courier business has been delivering some of Robertsons' Remedies locally."

Denny looked a little pale. "Well, you're right," he said. "We do deliver their products. I've never met them, but we've been delivering their stuff for the last five years or so. They sell everywhere in the Bakersfield area − though they ship out of Fresno."

He stopped and thought for a minute. "And I'm going to be frank with you. Jason Willard, the agent who's been making my life a living hell, wouldn't tell me the name of the shipper he suspected had been having its packages opened and tampered with in the last few months. But I think it was probably Robertsons' Remedies. After I turned the records over to Willard, I figured maybe I ought to poke around in them myself. Well, as it turned out, an amazing number of packages had been diverted without me really noticing what was going on."

"I see," Jupiter said. "So you must have some standard way for a customer to change the delivery address of  a shipment after the item is ordered."

"That's right," said Denny. "In the case of Robertsons' Remedies, once you place an order, their fulfillment company up in Fresno puts your order in a package with your address on it, and then one of my drivers picks it up in Fresno. He brings it back to the warehouse where it's sorted according to the delivery area, and then it gets loaded onto the specified truck. But if you decide you want the package delivered somewhere else, after you place the order but before it's actually out for delivery, you just log in to your account on our website, enter the order number, and request a different delivery address. The  only difference is that the package would have to be signed for in that case."

"I see," said Jupiter. "And does this happen often?"

"Hardly ever," Denny said. "But when I went back and checked the last few months, it turned out it was happening a *lot*,  and almost all the diverted packages had been from Robertsons' Remedies. But here's the strange thing – at least considering what you just told me. In every single case the person who was listed as having changed the address on the Robertsons' packages was Dave Robertson himself!"

Up to this point Pete, Bob, and Mallory had all been totally silent, but when Denny Ackers said his uncle's name, Pete almost squawked. "You're kidding, right?" he said.

Denny looked at him quite sympathetically. "Unfortunately not. Though to tell you the truth, if it hadn't been for Jason Willard's investigation – if I had just seen the list of diverted packages with Dave Robertson's name on them – I wouldn't have thought anything of it. After all, the guy owns the company that's shipping the packages to begin with!"

"That's true," said Jupiter. "It's very clever, actually." He sounded a little glum to Pete. "I can promise you that Mr. Robertson definitely *isn't* the person who's been diverting those packages, but since it's been done online by someone who knew the password, it's going to be mighty hard to find out who actually did it."

"It sure is," Pete said. "And I was so sure it must be Franklin Weaver!"

"Franklin Weaver?" asked Denny. "Why would *he* be doing something like that?"

"He wouldn't," Jupiter said firmly. "Pete just heard a nasty rumor about him from one of his cousins. We knew it couldn't really be true."

Belatedly but enthusiastically, Pete said, "Yeah, that's right!" – to which Denny said, "I've always liked old Franklin. And my kids think his amusement park is great. The oldest one is finally old enough to ride on the Nemesis. He's going to be there tonight, actually."

"Really?" Pete said.

He was just about to go on and ask Denny if *he* thought The Nemesis was haunted when Jupiter said, "We have one last question for you, if you're willing. Your brother said that this Jason Willard had started to blackmail you – but then he said that you wouldn't put it that way yourself. What did he mean by that, exactly?"

Denny smiled for the first time since they had gotten to his office.

"That's Cueball for you," he said. "Ever since he got arrested as a teenager for getting drunk and eating some oranges in a local orange grove, he's had a real poor opinion not only of the police but of every single person who works for the government or any of its agencies. He can't believe that a single person in a position of so-called "authority" can possibly be anything but an enemy.

"All he meant," Denny continued, "was that Jason Willard warned me that if I didn't cooperate with the Health and Safety Commission by letting them see my records, he'd have to make a formal request, through legal channels. I also had to sign a piece of paper saying that I'd told him everything I knew, and that if I'd knowingly lied, I could be prosecuted. No one likes to bullied like that, but it isn't exactly blackmail!"

"I see," said Jupiter. "Well, thank you very much for talking to us. When your brother asked us to visit you, he seemed to think we might be able to help you – but in the end, it was you who helped us."

"Glad to do it," said Denny. There were handshakes all around, and soon Pete was standing outside the warehouse with Mallory, Bob, and Jupiter, feeling even more dazed than he'd felt the night before. Although Pete wasn't always as swift on the uptake as he wished he were when things suddenly changed in a Three Investigators case, this time he had seen the sudden curve balls flying by him even before his friends pointed them out.

Which they did now.

"From what Denny told us," Jupiter said, "it seems likely that by now the Health and Safety Commission has launched a criminal investigation into Pete's aunt and uncle."

But Mallory topped this. "I can't believe that Cueball may have been one of the teenagers Charlie Robertson had arrested at the Golden Globe that night!" she said.

10

## Daman Does His Stuff

Thirty minutes later they were back in their hotel, sitting in Pete and Jupiter's room. Although Bob was extremely aware that two of them were going to have to hustle to get to the meeting with Daman Duwalia at Tehachapi Biogen, it still wasn't clear which of the them would be going. Still, Bob suspected it would be him and Pete.

When Pete had suggested they *all* should go, Jupiter had explained that Daman had specifically asked for just two of them – that he had thought that all four showing up might raise the suspicions of the team at Tehachapi Biogen, and *if* it did have anything to conceal, raising its suspicions would be unwise.

Jupiter had also told them that Daman was planning to claim – if he had to – that the two young people who were with him at the meeting were two young fans who had won a contest giving them the right to spend the day with him. Pete was psyched; since he *was* a fan, he'd have no trouble pretending, but since Bob's acting skills were somewhere between terrible and nonexistent, he felt quite worried at the prospect.

In any case, Jupiter seemed to have convinced himself that even though the investor's meeting would probably only take an hour or an hour and a half, he and Mallory should use the time to go to City Hall to check out the legal record of all the people who had owned the Golden Globe Citrus Grove. Since today was a Saturday, City Hall was closing at 2:00, so the only time to go to the land records office would be now.

Mallory said she'd like to see if City Hall had an old newspaper archive she could poke around in to see if she could discover the identity of the three teenagers who had been arrested in the grove by Dave Robertson's father.

"It *might* have been Cueball," she said to the others, "but I can't see why he wouldn't have mentioned it, if it *was*. After all, I did tell him that Pete's aunt and uncle owned a citrus grove."

"That's true," said Jupiter, "But I don't think you mentioned the name of the grove, and when Cueball started talking about visiting Franklin Weaver's amusement park, you never got back to it."

"Still," Mallory said. "I'm sure if I'd

mentioned the name of the Robertsons' citrus grove and it *was* the place he'd gotten arrested, he would have told us."

Bob had to agree with that. Cueball had seemed like a real straight shooter – though his Three Investigators experience had proven to Bob that almost everyone had something to hide.

That aside, the meeting with Denny Ackers had left them all feeling shaky, because it had literally never occurred to any of them before this morning that Pete's aunt and uncle might end up as the subjects of a criminal investigation.

"I still don't get it," Pete said. "How could the government imagine that Uncle Dave and Aunt Lilli would want to harm their own business? If whoever has been diverting their company's packages has been putting something into the Valley fever supplement, it pretty much *has* to be someone who wants to destroy their business!"

"I agree," said Jupiter. "But the more I see of what the government can get up to, the more I wonder whether simple logic ever comes into their equations. At least what Denny Ackers told us proves that someone really *is* trying to hurt your aunt and uncle's business! Someone – or maybe several someones. Perhaps several someones who work at Tehachapi Biogen. If my theory is right and  what's happening to Pete's aunt and uncle is because their Valley fever product is a potential competitor to the startup's product in development, then presumably everyone who's heavily invested has a motive to damage or destroy the Robertsons' reputation – or maybe their entire company."

Jupiter stopped and thought for a moment. "I actually think the scientists and researchers who are developing the various products would also have a motive. They'll clearly become very rich if even one of their new drugs is successful. They may not have invested their own money, but it *is* their work, and they must have an agreement with the investors that would give them a significant share of the company stock when the company goes public."

This struck Bob as an interesting observation – one that hadn't occurred to him.

"One other thing I'd like to look into, on my end," Jupiter added, "is who, exactly, owns the Roundup. If someone has been using it as a drop-point for diverted packages, that someone almost certainly has an in with the management or the owner – and may even be the owner himself."

That hadn't occurred to Bob either, but now that Jupiter said it, he could see that he must be right.

"But if that's true," he said, "it should be incredibly easy to find out who's behind this!"

"It would seem so, " Jupiter said. "But so far, nothing seems really easy about this case. Anyway, Bob, you and Pete had better get going. You should probably walk. It's only a few blocks from here to Tehachapi Biogen, and since Daman will be arriving in his car, you can ask him to drive you out to the Golden Globe afterwards. I don't know how Mallory and I are going to get there, but I guess we'll take our bikes again. Just give me and Mallory a call when you're out of the meeting, and we'll figure out what to do then."

And with that, they split up into two teams, with Pete and Bob heading toward Tehachapi Biogen, side by side on the sidewalk. Bob remembered that the last time they'd walked like this, a piano had crashed to the ground twenty-five feet in front of them.

Pete must have been remembering it, too, because he asked, "So, did your father like the Writer's Dice?"

"I think so," Bob said. "We sure laughed a lot."

When they got to the building they were heading for, they'd hardly even had time to look around when a  horn honked and a  low-slung and fancy red convertible with its top down, pulled up to the curb and parked. Daman Duwalia climbed out.

He wore a long-sleeved white silk shirt, open at the neck, and a pair of gray linen trousers. The sun had darkened his olive skin, and his curly black hair looked completely tidy. He'd been driving for an hour and a half with the top down, but the wind hadn't dared to mess with it.

When he took off his expensive sunglasses, Bob could see his dark brown eyes. His smile was dazzling. He was every inch a movie star. Bob was half-afraid a panic would ensue, that people passing on the street would recognize him. It was true that people were staring – at the convertible and at the man who had gotten out of it. But no one stopped and came over to ask for an autograph. Bob hoped it stayed that way.

"Hey, Bob," Daman said. "Hey, Pete. I thought Mallory was going to be here. Not that I'm not glad to see you two!"

"Jupiter and Mallory decided to go to City Hall while it was still open. To do some research about the case. It's great to see you, too!" Pete said. "Jupiter said you were working on a movie about Bakersfield or something!"

"Well, I'm in development on one," Daman said. "We haven't actually chosen Bakersfield as the final location, but we're seriously considering it. There's this place I go to when I want to get away – near Lake Isabella, about an hour east of here. The route takes me right by Bakersfield, so I've explored the city a bit. That's how I found your aunt and uncle's orange grove!

"But what I mainly do is hang out at the Roundup. It's a great country western bar. Even though I can tell that people sometimes recognize me, no one has ever bothered me. Everyone's just there to have a good time."

"So what's your movie about, exactly?" asked Pete.

Bob was starting to feel anxious about delivering Daman to the investors' meeting on time, but Daman seemed in no rush to get moving. He stood easily, smiling, as if they had all the time in the world.

"Well, it's set in the present day, and it's pretty serious," said Daman. "It's about the way a lot of working class men and women have been shoved to the sidelines in an America their grandparents mostly built. I'm supposed to play a sort of carpet bagger – an Indian guy with a lot of money and very little sense who comes into a crumbling city, but who learns to respect the people who already live there."

"That sounds great," said Pete.

Bob glanced at his watch, then showed it to Daman. It was closing in on one o'clock.

"We'd better be getting inside," he said.

"Yes," Daman said. "We don't want to be late."

They opened the glass doors and entered the lobby. The cool air soothed Bob's jangled nerves. As they headed for the staircase to the second floor, Bob asked impulsively, "You don't happen to know who owns The Roundup, do you?"

"It's funny you should ask that," Daman said. "I *don't* know who owns it, actually. But I do know it belongs to a consortium of investors – ten or fifteen wealthy men. I was given the opportunity to buy a piece, but I was an idiot and didn't do it."

Oh, no, Bob thought. If The Roundup was owned by a consortium, then it might not be easy at *all* to find out who had authorized taking delivery of the diverted packages.

They were almost to the second floor

when Daman said, "Remind me what it is that you want me to find out at this meeting?"

"What would be most helpful," Bob said, "is if you could discover who, exactly, has put up the money for the startup. Jupiter's theory is that if what's happening to Pete's aunt and uncle is because their Valley fever product is a potential competitor to the startup's product in development, then presumably everyone who's heavily invested has a motive to damage or destroy the Robertsons' reputation – or maybe their entire company."

"O.K." Daman said. "Got it. There may be some real bad guys here, playing mild-mannered scientists, so my role is to play a Hindi-speaking actor interested in investing in a biotech startup whose lead scientists also speak Hindi. That shouldn't be too hard. I had to learn  something about investments when I made a ton of money in the *Time Twist* movies. I'm investing in my own new movie, actually."

Daman seemed very relaxed and happy – happy to be in Bakersfield, happy to have made investments he thought he could count on, happy to be able to help The Three Investigators. He had managed to remain a decent and authentic person in spite of his celebrity and his success. Bob thought it was interesting that he'd been drawn to a story about a working class city like Bakersfield. To most people, an obvious star like Daman Duwalia would seem to belong over the Tejon Pass in Los Angeles, not here.

At the top of the stairs, Bob saw the entrance to Tehachapi Biogen. Daman walked confidently forward, a little ahead of Bob and Pete. Bob felt a little like a small yacht in the wake of an ocean liner. He could almost feel the waves that Daman made.

The receptionist today was a middle-aged Indian woman. From the minute she saw Daman, her face registered total shock, and as they approached the counter, she dissolved into something very much like giggles.

"You're … you're Daman Duwalia?" she said, as if she were uncertain.

"Yes," Daman said winningly, stretching out a hand to shake hers. "I'm very pleased to meet you." Bob could see that the woman didn't want to let go. "We're here for the investors' meeting." He freed his hand.

"You're just in time," the woman said. "It's down the hall in Conference Room 12."

"Thank you," Daman said, and they were off. There seemed to be no need for Daman to pretend that he and Pete were fans who had won some sort of contest, and for that Bob was grateful. He and Pete followed Daman down the hall to a room with clouded glass windows. A metal stanchion held a carefully lettered sign that read Tehachapi Biogen, Investors' Meeting, 1 pm.

Daman opened the door and the three of them walked in. Daman's entrance created quite a stir, Bob thought. Everyone turned to look at the late arrival. Bob counted eight men and five women, all of them wearing business clothes. Not only was Daman dressed more casually than anyone else, but Bob could see he was generally recognized. But though people smiled at him, no one said anything, and the three of them found seats in the last row. Bob was sure that having a famous actor among them made all the other investors feel quite smug.

Almost as soon as Bob and the others were seated, two Indian men and a white woman entered the room and sat behind a front table whose legs were shielded by red crepe.

"Good afternoon," one of the men said, "and thank you for coming. I'm Ashaan Chakrabati and these are my colleagues Advik Chopra and Mildred Gaines. Ms. Gaines is our Chief Financial Officer. Dr. Chopra will address the science and Ms. Gaines will address the economics. I'm sure when you hear more about who we are and what we're doing, you'll see that we are a premier investment for the 21st century."

Chakrabati and Chopra wore white lab coats and Ms. Gaines wore a blue pantsuit. All three of them looked very nerdy.

Chakrabati sat back and Dr. Chopra began. He gave a brief history of the company's founding and went on to explain what it was they were trying to achieve. If one of their formulas was aimed at Valley fever, he didn't come right out and say it. Soon enough Bob was lost in a fog of scientific terms. He couldn't follow the argument and as he tried to figure out what one sentence meant, Dr. Chopra was on to the next. It was incredibly dull and delivered in an unexcited monotone that trusted that the facts alone would be sufficient to convince the audience.

Bob glanced over at Pete and Daman. They both looked as if they were somehow following what was going on, and though Bob hardly saw how they could have been, his own fogginess was giving him plenty of time to worry, once again, about ever having promised

Pete's mother that The Three Investigators would help her sister's family.

It wasn't just that the whole thing continued to be so nebulous – which at least began with "n", Bob thought wryly, and therefore might be of use if this whole episode ever came to anything! – it was also that it really didn't satisfy him as a *writer*. As a writer, he had gotten used to showing the way in which A caused B and B in turn caused C. But this whole case was more like real life; it was all connected by conjunctions! There was A *and* B *and* C, but you often had no idea how they connected until after they were over – if then! Maybe that was what made life in general so boring to people who hadn't learned to be logical and think critically, Bob reflected.

He consoled himself with the thought that the presentation couldn't go on forever. Or maybe it could! But finally, after about twenty minutes, Dr. Chopra sat back and crossed his arms, looking satisfied, and Ms. Gaines started speaking. She asked if everyone had been given a copy of the Tehachapi Biogen prospectus and handed it out to those who didn't have one – which included Daman. As she began talking, the scientific terms were replaced with financial terms. There was a PowerPoint presentation. If anything, this was even more droningly boring, though Bob was aware that a number of the investors had perked right up when the numbers started flashing.

When Ms. Gaines was finished, Dr. Chakrabati opened the floor to questions, most of which, as far as Bob could ascertain, seemed to translate to "How much money will I make?" Bob thought he couldn't stand any more when all of a sudden it was over. The people in the meeting jumped to their feet smiling and soon were talking to one another or thanking the three panel members and leaving.

Daman stood as well. "Stay here," he said to Bob and Pete. Bob watched as Daman walked confidently to the table and shook hands with Chakrabati, Chopra, and Gaines. Bob couldn't hear what Daman was saying, but he could easily see the effect he was having on the two scientists and the CFO. Their eyes were riveted on his face. Whether it was because they recognized him and knew who he was, or because he was just being Daman Duwalia was impossible to tell. But Bob could see how easily and swiftly Daman had managed to charm the three of them.

He made large sweeping gestures with his hands. He laughed easily. He leaned forward confidentially. Their eyes were wide, their faces fixed in admiration. It was amazing watching him work. He was hypnotizing them. He had the same effect on them that he had on his global audiences when he appeared on screen. Finally, he shook their hands once again, pivoted, and returned to where Bob and Pete were sitting.

"That went well," he said.

"It sure looked that way from here," Pete said. "What happened?"

"I talked to the scientists in Hindi," Daman said, "not all the time, of course, because I got the sense that the CFO spoke only English and I didn't want to be rude. But they knew who I was, which worked to my advantage."

"I'd think everyone would know who you were," Pete said.

"The Indian community is especially proud of members of the diaspora who do well," Daman said. "I told them I was thinking of investing a great deal of money in their company, but only if I could get a hands-on view of the lab. They said they were impressed that I'd come to Bakersfield rather than one of their investor meetings in Los Angeles. I told them I'd just discovered them and didn't want to waste any time."

"Wow," Bob said. "Did you tell them you had a scientific background?"

"They asked me that, and I simply said that I'd be able to tell a lot by the way the place was set up and by talking to some of the researchers. So Dr. Chakrabati is taking me back there. At first they said that no unauthorized people were allowed, but I convinced him."

"What will you be looking for?" Pete asked.

"I don't really care about the lab at all," Daman said, "but I have the sense that if I can talk to Chakrabati in his natural environment – and away from money people – he might be a lot more relaxed and let his guard down. Especially if we're talking in Hindi."

"So what do you plan to do?" Bob asked.

"I'll ask him about his major investors," Daman said, "which is what you wanted me to find out. But I'll also try to pin him down about this medicine for Valley fever that he's working on. And I'll just let the conversation go where it goes. It may lead in interesting directions."

"O.K.," Bob said. "Good luck. We'll wait for you downstairs in the lobby."

Dr. Chakrabati was lingering at the door

to the conference room and Daman went back to meet him. As the two of them walked down the corridor and into Tehachapi Biogen's reception area, Bob and Pete followed them, keeping a safe distance.

Bob said as they clattered down the stairs to the lobby, "Daman certainly seems to know what he's doing."

Pete nodded enthusiastically. "I could tell he was into it," he said.

They sat on a bench in the lobby under the branches of a large potted ficus tree. It was a public place of sorts, though they were the only ones in it, and Bob was glad to have somewhere to wait, out of the blast furnace of early afternoon in downtown Bakersfield.

When Daman finally reappeared, sauntering down the stairs, he glowed all over with the glee of a job well done. Bob could tell it wasn't that he was proud of himself as much as he was happy to have been able to help. Bob and Pete stood and walked toward him.

"How'd it go?" Pete asked.

"Dr. Chakrabati was very nice," Daman said. "Very forthcoming. I have absolutely no idea if what they're cooking up in there will work with Valley fever or with anything else for that matter. I'm just not smart or educated enough to know what the science part of what he told me will amount to. But I'm pretty sure he's got nothing to do with what you're investigating. In other words, it's almost a certainty that Tehachapi Biogen isn't behind the Health and Safety Commission's harassment of the Robertsons."

"How do you know?" Pete asked.

"Well, Daman said, "for one thing, the main investor in the company is an Indian billionaire who lives in Mumbai. He owns a controlling interest – or will, when it goes public – but he's been very stingy when it comes to profit-sharing – though he's been great at paying big salaries. And while he's finally opening up the investment opportunities to people like the ones who were here today – up to now, there's only been one investor other than the billionaire – neither Chakrabati nor any of the others has a particularly high stake in the outcome of their research.

"And then he told me a story about how, when they first opened up, almost the first thing that happened was that they got a visit from someone in the Safety Commission who grilled them about their bona fides. Chakrabati couldn't remember his name, but he said he was a Hispanic guy who read them the riot act and told them they better not cut any corners. Chakrabati hates the guy. It's impossible for me to believe he or anyone else in the company would have anything to do with the Commission.

"So it's my opinion that whoever's behind the attack on the Robertsons, it isn't the people working for Tehachapi Biogen. I quite liked Chakrabati and everyone he introduced me to. It was fun speaking Hindi. I don't get to speak it very often."

Bob thought for a moment and then said, "Did you happen to learn who the only investor other than the billionaire was?"

"I did, actually," said Daman. "Chakrabati said that the guy who owns this building – some guy named Franklin Weaver – was allowed to invest in early shares of the company. It seems that he'd had Valley fever when he was a kid – and Tehachapi Biogen really wanted to be in this building!"

"Wow!" said Pete. "That's amazing that you learned that! Jupiter's going to be thrilled! He's had his eye on Franklin Weaver right from the start."

Bob agreed, and as he looked at Daman, he wondered what it would be like to walk through the world the way he did – to have the air part around you in hushed silence, to have every eye in the room on you, to have people become indiscreet just because they were standing in your presence It might be a rush, he thought, but in the end it was probably better to be a lot more invisible, if you wanted to investigate something.

"Well, I'm glad I got *something* useable," said Daman. "So let's get going. You can call Jupiter and Mallory from my car, and then we'll head out to Pete's aunt and uncle's place."

Daman's convertible was a **BMW** with leather seats, a steeply slanted windshield, and a powerful sound system. Bob was a bit stunned by its opulence. It was really designed for just two people. Pete got the front seat and Bob squeezed into the back, where he sat sideways, his feet up on the seat.

Once there, he called Mallory, who handed her phone to Jupiter so that Bob could tell him what Daman had said about the scientists at Tehachapi Biogen, as well as the owners of the Roundup. Jupiter sounded disappointed on both counts – but the news about Franklin Weaver bucked Jupiter up at once. He confirmed that he and Mallory would bicycle out to the Golden Globe Citrus Grove and meet Daman and his passengers there.

Daman pulled away from the curb and headed down 20th Street – one-way headed west. He turned on F Street and took it all the way south past Bakersfield High down to California Avenue. Daman certainly seemed to know his way around Bakersfield. He explained that this was a major east-west route through the city, and they were now headed east toward the Robertsons' place.

Daman clearly loved to drive. He had one arm on the door and one on the steering wheel, and he burst out from stoplights with a sense of excitement. But he soon timed the stoplights so that he could keep up a steady speed. The rush of air felt good to Bob. As they crossed Route 204, California Avenue became East California Avenue. Daman had lost his timing and they were hitting stoplights with regularity.

As they came up on Mt. Vernon Avenue, Bob could see the light turn yellow, but Daman, probably frustrated at the number of times they had already stopped, seemed to think he could get through. He stepped on the gas. He wasn't speeding, and was entirely within his rights, but Bob suddenly saw a car coming right at them in the middle of the intersection. The driver was heading north on Mt. Vernon and had jumped the light.

"Look out!" Bob yelled. He put his hands over his ears as though that might avert the crash.

The oncoming driver veered to the left, just missing the back end of the BMW. Brakes screeched as he lost control and rammed up on the sidewalk. A trash can went flying as the driver hit a light stanchion. Bob heard the smash of glass and the crumpling of metal.

Even though Daman hadn't been at fault, he immediately pulled to the curb and jumped out. So did Bob and Pete. They ran back across the intersection where cars were stopped and drivers sat gawking. Bob heard a siren in the distance. The other car wasn't badly damaged. Only its left headlight had been smashed and its bumper crumpled. But Bob could see that the driver was very shaken up. He sat dazed behind the wheel, bleeding from a cut on his forehead. He was an older man, with white hair, wearing a business suit. He looked vaguely familiar.

"Oh my gosh," Pete said. "It's Franklin Weaver! Mr. Weaver, are you all right?" Franklin Weaver the Third turned his head in Pete's direction, apparently trying to focus.

Oh, no, thought Bob – and not merely because there'd been an accident. That was bad, of course, but what *really* seemed bad just then was that the accident had happened to the man Daman himself had just moved into the category of prime suspect!

# 11

## The Case Moves
## Backwards and Forward

**A**n hour and a half before, as Bob and Pete had been setting off on foot to meet Daman at Tehachapi Biogen, Jupiter and Mallory were unlocking their bikes to head to City Hall.

"You know, Jupiter," Mallory said. "I really think we might want to call Cueball if we're actually going to meet up with Daman and Pete and Bob at the Robertsons'. I don't mind biking just about anywhere, but it's not much fun around Bakersfield. When we were in San Francisco we hired a car service."

"I know," Jupiter said. "In fact, I was thinking about that last night."

"You know what else I've been thinking about?" asked Mallory. "About Pete's paper on Stephen Decatur. I was thinking that even though Lilliana Robertson is Pete's mother's sister, she and her husband wouldn't really understand why Pete thought Decatur was so great. I mean, he and his aunt and uncle don't really have much in common. Like me and Skinny."

Jupiter suddenly remembered the moment when Bob had first described Mallory – at a time when he had met her and Jupiter hadn't. Actually, Pete had met her, too, by then, but he had learned she was Skinny Norris's cousin at the same time that Jupiter had – and he'd let out a yelp of astonishment.

As far as he could remember, Jupiter had responded by pointing out that even within a nuclear family, there were often big genetic variations, and Pete had said something like, "I don't know, Jupe. Those two being cousins is the most amazing example of genetic variation you're ever going to run into. I think you'd actually *like* this girl."

"I have no reason not to," Jupiter had said. "But I doubt we have very much in common."

"I wouldn't be so sure," said Bob. "I think you might have a lot more in common than you think."

"Only time will tell," Jupiter had said.

Well, time *had* told, thought Jupiter. "You and Skinny are a special case," he said. "But I know what you mean about the Robertsons."

They buckled on their helmets and started off down the streets of Bakersfield. The traffic was steady, and Jupiter found it unnerving to be constantly passed by large heaps of speeding metal. Back in Rocky Beach, you could ride your bike relatively unimpeded, but here it was dangerous, he thought. Maybe Mallory was right, and when the time came to go back to the Golden Globe, he should ask her to call Cueball.

Of course, he was well aware that motorcycles could be dangerous, too, but that actually wasn't why he hadn't jumped at the chance to  get a ride on a Harley. Why *did* he find the idea unappealing? he wondered as he pedaled.

Well, in the first place, although Cueball and Buzz and Rooster and Knuckles seemed like decent human beings, he had just met them yesterday, and even if he had known them a lot better than he did, he still wouldn't have wanted to jump on a bike behind one of them, grip him around the middle, and hang on for dear life.

Gripping someone from behind on a motorcycle was a pretty intimate thing, after all. Of course, these particular motorcycles *did* have that extra seat cushion – he thought it was called a pillion – which would keep him from actually being pressed up against whoever he was riding with. So maybe he should reconsider.

Although it was strange to think that he might be subject to the same prejudices all too many other people had, he had to admit that, to him, riding a motorcycle was associated with being a member of the working classes – something he didn't think of himself as being. Which was really pretty funny, since his aunt and uncle owned a salvage yard, and he lived in a house just behind it. If that didn't make him a member of the working classes, it was hard to know what would!

Boy, it really *was* hot. It seemed to be frying Jupiter's brain more every minute – and the worst thing about *that* was that he had been looking forward to having a really solid talk with Mallory about the case. In fact, that was the real reason he'd decided to send Pete and Bob off to meet Daman Duwalia, while he and she went to City Hall. Not so much because he needed her research skills on this assignment, but because he wanted her to help him analyze the various possibilities as to what was going on with the Robertsons. The summer before, when they'd been in San Francisco staying at a hostel, he'd found one particular private discussion they'd had invaluable.

Putting that thought aside, Jupiter returned to his prior one – the one about the working classes. The fact was, since his father and mother had both been astronomers and his father had taught at a university in Canada, while his aunt and uncle *did* own and operate a salvage yard, he himself had always had a foot in two very different camps. He liked that, and thought it had served him really well.

But then class in America had always been a pretty funny thing. Not funny as in hah hah, but funny as in strange, Jupiter thought. After all, the essence of the American dream was that whatever class you might start off in, you could get to another, higher up. As long as you used the talents you were born with, and were willing to work hard, there was – theoretically – nothing you couldn't achieve.

Just then, Jupiter finally sighted City Hall, and soon he and Mallory had fastened their bikes to a bike rack and were making their way to the room which held the land records. He knew he and the others had to do their best to try to get a handle on something that might help the Robertsons.

After all, Pete was as much a part of Jupiter's own family as Uncle Titus and Aunt Mathilda, and if his mother's sister was harmed, Pete would be, too. Even so, Jupiter was beginning to get the feeling that there were simply too many nit-picky details – and too many possible leads – for Jupiter and the others to sort things out in an even halfway timely manner. They could hardly spend the whole summer looking into this one case – at least, while he supposed they *could*, he, for one, didn't want to!

As they settled down at one of the big tables in the records room, Mallory said, "You know, before we start poking around in the filing cabinets, I'd like to look up whatever I can find on the Internet about Franklin Weaver the First. I know you're hoping that the villains in this case are connected with Tehachapi Biogen – but I've been thinking that if Weaver the Third wanted to buy the Robertsons' land five years ago, he might still  want to buy it now, and if he did, putting the Robertsons out of business would be a good way to start. He's got a lot of connections, and maybe even enough  power to twist the arm of a government agency like the Health and Safety Commission. I know you've considered this before, but maybe we should  consider it again."

"That's fine with me," said Jupiter. "Go ahead and see what you can find."

Mallory took out her laptop, opened it up, and after searching for a while with no success, finally found an obituary of Franklin Weaver the First. It was a photograph of part of a page of the Lindsay *Clarion*, which had been stored on microfiche.

"Boy, am I lucky to have found this," Mallory said. "This paper has clearly never been digitized."

The text was blurry and smudged but she and Jupiter could make it out. Franklin Weaver, born 1891, the son of Clyde Weaver and Ida Louise (White) Weaver had died August 26, 1942 of complications of Valley fever. "Proprietor of Weaver's General Store. Survived by his wife of 24 years Beatrice and his son Franklin Weaver II," the text said.

"That's right," Jupiter agreed. "Billy Taylor said that *our* Franklin Weaver's grandfather had died of Valley fever. Frankie's father."

"In 1942," Mallory said. "Wally and Charlie had just begun serving in the Army in World War II. Why didn't Frankie serve? Did Wally say? I don't remember."

"He must have had a deferment of some kind," Jupiter said. "At least I suppose so. Is there any more information in the obituary?"

Mallory read to the end. "It says here

that he owned a holding company called Kern County Fruit and that he owned a patchwork of citrus groves throughout the Valley. Kern County Fruit is a pretty colorless name for a man who was about to begin a dynasty of Franklin Weavers."

"He probably didn't want to call attention to himself, at least in business," Jupiter said. "His grandson didn't use Weaver in the name of his business either – it's just the Citrus and Carnival Ranch."

"That may be so," Mallory said. "But from the way he was boasting when we ran into him at Tehachapi Biogen, he's not hiding his light under a bushel. Oh, wait, look at this. It's some sort of human interest story about Franklin Weaver's wife and son. It's dated about a year after his death."

"Franklin Weaver's son would be Wally's Frankie," said Jupiter. "Well, what does it say?"

Mallory read it through twice. "Wow. It's quite a story. It's actually a follow-up about the making of *The Grapes of Wrath*. It seems that the movie was considered so important to the locals who had appeared in it – and also those who hadn't – that the reporter pitched a sort of Three Years Later story, and had it approved. Wally was right. It seems that Frankie was crushed not to have gotten cast, so to make him feel better, his father had promised him his own orange grove when he turned 21. One of the holding company's citrus groves. When he was still a senior in high school, Franklin II used to go there and walk on it, as if he already owned it.

"Then high school ended and the war started. Frankie's old nemeses, Wally Tate and Charlie Robertson, had been drafted and went off to fight, while Frankie, who had flat feet and family connections, got to stay home and start making money. Of course, it doesn't say that in the article," Mallory added, smiling. "But what it *does* say is that, before Frankie turned 21, his father had died of Valley fever, and when his financial affairs turned out to be messy, Frankie's mother had had to let the bank foreclose on a number of her husband's properties – including the orange grove Frankie's father had promised him."

"Hhhm," said Jupiter. "Is that the end of the story?"

"Not quite," said Mallory. "It says that although Franklin II had been heartbroken when this happened, there was nothing he could do but resolve to make a lot of money and buy the land back. If Frankie could pay more than market price, the land would be his again."

Looking at Jupiter gravely, Mallory said, "I know you're not a betting man, but how much do you want to bet that the parcel Frankie was promised by his father is the parcel the Robertsons now own?"

"Not a single penny piece," Jupiter said. "Though we'd better check to make certain."

It took almost forty minutes, and a lot of checking and cross-checking, but eventually Mallory and Jupiter stood in front of a City Hall copy machine, copying the page in the book of records.

And while this seemed to Jupiter an indisputable breakthrough in the case, neither he nor Mallory could come up with a truly plausible reason why Franklin III would have wanted to purchase the very same parcel of land his recently-widowed grandmother had lost. As Mallory pointed out, it wasn't as if there was treasure hidden beneath the land.

"Anyway," she added. "Since City Hall is closing soon, I don't think we're going to have time to do any checking in the archives about the three teenagers arrested in the Golden Globe. Why don't we find somewhere else with Wi-Fi so I can get back on the Internet and see if I can find out anything else online? Maybe I can also research the owner of the Roundup."

Jupiter was just about to agree to this proposal, when he heard a mild buzzing he guessed must be Mallory's phone. She opened it, punched it, said "Oh, hi, Bob," then handed the phone to Jupiter.

"Jupiter, it's Bob." Bob's voice sounded thin and jumbled with traffic noise.

"Where are you?" Jupiter asked.

"On 20th Street outside Tehachapi Biogen," Bob said. "Daman did his work, and I'm sorry to say that he strongly believes that none of the people who work there have any incentive to mess with the Robertsons. Of course he might be wrong."

"He might be," said Jupiter. "But he probably isn't. That takes us back to square one. But at least we can cross off that possibility. Did you find out anything else?"

"Daman told us that The Roundup is owned by a consortium of investors," Bob said. "As many as fifteen different people. That's going to make it pretty tricky to figure out who gave instructions to take delivery of the diverted packages. On the plus side, Daman learned that Franklin Weaver is one of the investors in Tehachapi Biogen. There aren't very many, but I guess he basically demanded to be allowed to own a piece of the company in exchange for letting it rent offices in his building."

Now that *was* news, Jupiter thought. When you put it together with what he and Mallory had just learned about Franklin Weaver's father having wanted to purchase the very same parcel of land he had been promised by his own father, it suddenly seemed to suggest that maybe, despite what Mallory had said, and he had agreed with, there really *was* some sort of treasure hidden beneath the land!

"That alone was worth the price of admission," Jupiter said to Bob.

"I agree," said Bob. "Daman's going to drive me and Pete to the Golden Globe now. His car is tiny. It's a convertible with just a single real seat. I'm perched on a sort of shelf right now. Can you guys get to the Robertsons on your bikes?"

"If we have to — though I'm getting more and more interested in Cueball's offer to act as our chauffeurs. Still, we'll manage," Jupiter said.

He and Mallory finished packing up their gear, retrieved their bicycles, and headed back east on California Street toward the Golden Globe. As East California Street approached Mt. Vernon Avenue, Jupiter could see it was a major intersection – two lanes of divided traffic headed east-west meeting two lanes of divided traffic headed north-south. There were two traffic lights and a lot of snarled traffic. When they got closer, Jupiter was perturbed to see there'd been a minor traffic accident. Someone in a late-model maroon sedan had lost control and had run up on the sidewalk, hitting one of the traffic light stanchions.

It seemed to have happened only minutes before. The sedan had a smashed headlight and crumpled bumper, but it didn't look too serious. Drivers inched past, rubbernecking.

Jupiter and Mallory had come to a stop when he saw three people jump out of a convertible parked across the street and run to the sedan. Jupiter squinted in disbelief. They looked like Pete and Bob. He got off his bike and started pushing it toward the accident. What on earth – ?

Daman Duwalia seemed less astonished than Bob and Pete did.

"Hey, Jupiter," Daman said. "Hey, Mallory."

"We were just on our way to meet you," Jupiter said. "What happened?"

Bob quickly filled him in. "And the driver?" he said. "It's Franklin Weaver!"

That, to Jupiter, was considerably more surprising than running into Pete, Bob, and Daman. Franklin Weaver had gotten out of the car and was now apologizing profusely to Daman Duwalia. He looked stunned, even a little haggard. A cut on his forehead was bleeding.

"My foot just hit the gas!" he said. "I don't know what happened. I was in a hurry, yes, but – "

Jupiter could see at once that he was badly shaken, and that the accident had caused him to lose his natural reserve. Big adrenaline rushes were like that, putting all your senses on high alert, though they could also overwhelm you if they were too intense. They were the body's way of putting up a defense, mobilizing against danger.

Weaver was still running on. His normally imperious self was gone, especially in the presence of this handsome and obviously extremely wealthy young man. Clearly, Weaver saw Daman as a force to be reckoned with. Instead of blaming him for the accident – which Jupiter assumed Weaver would normally have done with just about anyone else – he kept apologizing.

"This is only my second accident," he said, "and I've been driving since I was a teenager. The other one was just like this, too, when I was in a hurry. I'm in a hurry now, and I still need to get there. I really do – " He faltered, looked at Daman earnestly, and suddenly sat down on the ground.

"Shock," Daman said, "and maybe a concussion. He wasn't wearing his seat belt. I'll call 911."

In a little while, a police cruiser and an ambulance pulled up, and Daman gave a statement as the medics strapped Weaver to a gurney and took him away. A tow truck came to remove Weaver's car, and the policeman directed traffic, and the whole scene looked like it was soon to return to normal.

Still, this whole event seemed incredibly strange to Jupiter – especially the fact that it had happened not long after he and Mallory had found out that Franklin Weaver's grandfather had not only once owned what was now the Robertsons land, but that Franklin the Second had wanted, and planned, to buy it back.

Jupiter didn't know yet why he'd never done so, but one thing he *did* know was that the time had come for  someone to call Cueball and ask him and his friends for a ride to the Golden Globe. When Jupiter asked Mallory to do that, she did, and  soon the two of them were riding their bikes back to The Oasis, while Daman and Pete and Bob followed in Daman's car.

The bikers were waiting at The Oasis, and to Jupiter's surprise, they had rustled up an extra set of helmets from somewhere or other. What was even more surprising was how interested Daman Duwalia seemed in Buzz and Rooster and Cueball and Knuckles. He said he was glad to meet them, then started eying them almost as if they were criminals in a lineup. Well, no, not that exactly.  More as if he were sitting in a theater watching actors in a play.

"Well, let's go, then," Cueball said – at which Daman said, "Who's riding with me?" And while Jupiter had fully intended to climb on the back of one of the Harleys for the trip to the Golden Globe, he found himself saying, "I will, if that's O.K."

"It's  perfect," said Daman. While Rooster handed out helmets to Pete, Bob, and Mallory, Jupiter  climbed into Daman's BMW, and soon the whole procession was heading for the Golden Globe, with Daman leading the way. Although Jupiter felt a bit chagrined that he hadn't followed through on his determination to take his first ride on a motorcycle, he also felt that he needed to get his thoughts about the case in order before he had to present them not just to the other Three Investigators, but also to Daman – and there was no doubt that would be easier in the front seat of a BMW than perched on the back of a Harley Davidson.

12

## An Unexpected Revelation

It was fifteen  minutes later, and as Pete climbed off the back of Cueball's Harley and onto the dust of his aunt and uncle's driveway, he felt simultaneously elated and unhappy. He thought the bikers were great, and although he'd been on the back of motorbikes before, he couldn't remember ever having had a smoother ride.

However, the longer this case went on, and the more people who got involved with trying to solve it, the more doubtful Pete began to feel about whether it would be worth all the time and energy they were expending on it. In terms of just days, or hours, it actually hadn't been that long since he had heard about the poisoned orange trees, but in terms of something more elusive, he felt as if it had been an eternity.

For one thing, though none of his friends had actually said this, by now Pete had gotten the feeling – at least sometimes! – that they would really rather be doing anything but what they were doing, in any place but here. While their cases weren't *always* fantastically exciting, Pete thought, with every one they'd ever had except for this one, they'd gotten to choose it for themselves. To choose it freely.

Even before Mallory had joined them, The Three Investigators had always taken the cases that interested them and left the other ones alone. In this case, however, it was clear, looking back on it, that he, Pete, should have shut his mother down right away when she first brought the subject up.

Of course, at that point, he and the others had thought that the main issue was the poisoned orange trees, and although they were as far from finding out who had poisoned them as ever, they had  uncovered something that was clearly entirely out of their league.

No one on earth could be expected to deal with what they'd uncovered – the diverting of packages in order to adulterate their contents – without the help of some government agency or other, Pete thought. But in this case, it was at least possible that a government agency was, itself, involved. The whole thing was a tangle even Mission Impossible wouldn't be able to untangle.

As the bikers, The Three Investigators, and Daman Duwalia all unloaded themselves from their vehicles and shook off the dust of the road, Pete saw that Mateo and Estevan were in the yard, hanging out near the makeshift stand whose doors were wide open, revealing the glowing orange pyramids of fruit. He waved at them. Mateo looked suitably impressed by Daman's car, as well as its driver.

"Daman Duwalia?" he said as though he couldn't believe his eyes.

"Hey, Mateo," Pete said. "Where's everybody?"

"Dad's at the lawyers," Mateo said, "and Mom and Gabriella are in town shopping. Me and Estevan are holding down the fort."

"You're not working?" Pete asked.

"Billy scheduled me to help out this morning, to open, and then he sent me home. I have to go back tonight because I'm running The Nemesis. Are you guys coming?"

"Maybe," Pete said. "But I don't think so. Anyway, Daman's going to be here for a while, but  the bikers aren't, so I've got to go say thanks to them, and goodbye. We'll see you in a bit."

But although Pete had only been absent from the main group for a minute or two, when he got back he found that in his absence,

Daman had started talking to the bikers about his new movie  – the one he'd said might be set in Bakersfield.

"No, really, I'd like your contact info," Daman was saying. "If the film gets off the ground, the director's going to be wanting to cast some genuine bikers. Not just  bikers, but locals from all walks of life. You guys would be perfect, seriously."

While Pete was amazed by this proposal, the bikers seemed a lot less so.

"I get you," said Rooster. "You want authentic local color."

"That's right," said Daman. "But not just that. We want people who can tell us when we're going wrong."

The bikers all nodded as if they understood perfectly – after which they all gave Daman their full names and phone numbers, which he programmed into his phone. And then they were gone again – though not before telling The Three Investigators that they'd be at The Roundup that evening, and that if they could help at all with the planned surveillance of Arsenio Santiago, they'd be happy to do it.

After they'd roared off on their Harleys, Pete waved to Mateo and Estevan to come over. "I guess you don't need to be introduced to *them*, but Daman, these are my cousins, Mateo and Estevan. Daman gets a shipment of your oranges every month," he said to his cousins.

"I'm pleased to meet you," Daman said.

Estevan grabbed a piece of scrap lumber and held it up, making the unusual sound that the retro-futuristic weapons in the *Time Twist* series made. Daman laughed.

"Can I get you some sodas or something?" Mateo asked.

"Sure," said Daman.

Mateo was back in a few minutes and invited Daman and The Three Investigators to sit around a table not far from the fruit stand – which he and Estevan had to keep manning.

Pete could see that Jupiter was eager to start a review of the case so far – and maybe even to tell him and Bob whatever he and Mallory had discovered at City Hall. But this was the first time the five of them had been together in a place where they could really talk since the end of the case on which they'd met Daman, so it startled Pete when Daman suddenly said, smiling, "So I hear that you and Califia Garcia-Williams are an item. I bumped into her at some theater thing, and she told me."

Instantly, Pete's face grew hot.

"Oh, she did?" he asked with a gulp.

"Califia was great to work with," Daman said. "And a real pro! She's got quite a career ahead of her."

Just then, a phone rang. Pete looked around and saw Bob taking his phone from his pocket. As he glanced at the caller ID, Bob's face lit up.

"Wally!" he said. "How are you? Are you in Rocky Beach?" He paused. "No, we're up at the Golden Globe again, hot on the trail of your old rival. At least I think so."

He quickly filled Wally in on where they were in their investigation, paying particular attention to all they'd learned about Franklin Weaver. Pete wanted to hear everything Wally was saying.

"Everyone here looks quite anxious," Bob said. "Is it O.K. if I put you on speakerphone?"

He hit a button and put the phone on the table. Everyone leaned forward to get closer.

"Hello, everyone!" Wally's thin voice said from across the width of California. "So are you going to get the miscreant?"

"We hope so," Jupiter said.

"Well, I'm glad," Wally said. "If anyone

239

deserved a bunch of bloodhounds nipping at his heels, it's − . Wait. I keep forgetting. It's not Frankie Weaver you're after. It's his son."

"That's right," Jupiter said.

"But it's Frankie I'm calling about," Wally said. "I just remembered something. I know I already told you that after Charlie and I got parts in *The Grapes of Wrath* and Frankie didn't, he was so angry that he said that he'd be happy to spend the rest of his life ruining ours."

A vendetta, Pete thought.

"You did tell us that," said Bob.

"Anyway, what I've just remembered is that not long after he said that, I ran into him one day when I was delivering ice to his house," Wally said. "That day, Frankie told me he didn't care about the stupid movie, anyway. We probably hadn't gotten paid for it, and be-sides we were just stupid working class kids who would probably have to work for the California Ice Company for the rest of our lives. But not him. No, he told me his father had promised him a really big present for his twenty-first birthday. Which wasn't very far away."

It was funny, Pete thought, how something that had happened to you when you were young could cast such a long shadow. Wally hadn't held a grudge exactly. It wasn't as if he'd spent his life trying to get back at Frankie Weaver. But it sounded as though the hurt he'd suffered all those years ago was still fresh in his mind – and as if Frankie Weaver really *had* held a grudge.

"He wouldn't tell me what it was," Wally went on, "though he clearly knew. He said he was going to put a present for himself in with the present from his father, and that, as a joke on me and Charlie, he was going to use a California Ice Company box to put it in."

"What did he mean?" Jupiter said. "A present for himself in with the present from his father?"

"I don't know," Wally said. "Frankie didn't always talk sense, especially when he was going on. But it occurred to me that Frankie's father died of Valley fever before Frankie ever turned 21, so he may never have even gotten the present his father had promised him. I've got so many memories rattling around in this old head of mine that I don't know if it will help you or not. But I thought I'd tell you anyway. When are you coming back to Rocky Beach?"

"In a day or so," Jupiter said. "As soon as we wind up this case. Or as soon as we aren't able to."

"I'll see you then," Wally said. "Isabella

sends her love."

"Goodbye, Wally," they all said, and Bob hung up.

"Let me get this straight," Daman said. "Your friend Wally knew the father of the man in the accident just now?"

"That's right," Jupiter said. "Frankie is Franklin Weaver the Second. The man who ran into the stanchion is Franklin Weaver the Third. And get this – while Mallory and I were at City Hall, she found an article online, dated 1942. A human interest story – a three-year follow-up to the release of *The Grapes of Wrath* – and it said that Wally's Frankie – the guy Wally was just talking about – had been promised an orange grove for his twenty-first birthday."

"A whole orange grove?" Pete asked incredulously.

"A whole orange grove," said Jupiter. "*That* was the present he wouldn't describe to Wally! But since his father owed a lot of money to a lot of banks when he died, some of his land was foreclosed on – including the parcel he'd promised to give his son. And guess what? That parcel was the piece of land we're all sitting on right now! Mallory and I made a copy of the deed at City Hall."

While Pete watched in astonishment, Jupiter hauled this out of his backpack and unfolded it.

"I'm totally gobsmacked," Pete said.

"I am, too," said Daman. "But if I'm following this story properly, the Franklin Weaver who lost out on the birthday present was the *father* of the man who was carted away in the ambulance."

"That's right," Jupiter said. "Which creates a pretty big problem for us. Because even though the fact that Franklin Weaver is an investor in Tehachapi Biogen gives him a motive for wanting to put the Robertsons out of business, it doesn't really explain why he would want to buy their land. And if he wants to put them out of business as a way to *force* them to sell their land, his motive would have to go back to something his father told him. But what?"

There was silence for a moment, until Bob spoke up. "Well, Wally just told us that Frankie was going to put a present for himself in with the present from his father, and that as a joke on him and Charlie, he was going to use a California Ice Company box. Just like the ice box Charlie himself used to bury some stuff under the barn."

"That really *is* possible," Jupiter said, sounding almost excited. "He clearly knew what land his father intended him to have. The article Mallory located said that, when he was still a senior in high school, Franklin II used to go there and walk on it, as if he already owned it. Maybe there really *is* treasure here somewhere, and Franklin Weaver the Third knows all about it from his father! "

Treasure! Pete thought. He was a fan of treasure. He looked at Jupiter in amazement. So did Daman.

"It seems you haven't lost your touch," he said. "You guys are great investigators. Listen, I wish I could stay, but I've got to go. I've got a two-hour ride back, and I'm supposed to go to a screening of the new film by a director who wants me for his next movie."

"So soon?" Pete said. "That's too bad."

"It's been fun talking," Daman said. "I hope I'll see you all again before too long. And be sure to let me know what happens."

"With Franklin Weaver the Third in the hospital," Jupiter said, "everything ought to be stable for a while. Tonight we're going to spy on Arsenio Santiago at The Roundup."

"Geez," Daman said. "I love the Roundup. I wish I could join you. Great line dancing."

They all walked Daman to his car.

"Thanks for everything," Pete said.

"I didn't do all that much," Daman said.

"Not true," Jupiter said. "By helping us eliminate Tehachapi Biogen as a suspect you helped a lot."

Daman got into his convertible and took off toward the highway, leaving a cloud of dust in his wake. As Pete, Bob, Mallory, and Jupiter walked to join Mateo and Estevan at the farm stand, a car drove up, discharging a Hispanic family – a mother, father, and a girl and a boy, about eight and nine years old. Mateo called out to them.

"Mr. Romero," he said. "Back so soon!"

"We can't get enough of your oranges, seriously," Mrs. Romero said.

While Mateo went to take care of them, the boy and girl ran over to the closed shed. The boy stood on tiptoes, put his hands to the sides of his eyes, and tried to look through the small windows of the garage-type door.

"It's all dark in there," he said. "Why is it closed up?" He seemed puzzled by the change. "This is where we always go."

"It's a long story," Pete said. "The stand's over there now." He pointed to where the boy's parents were talking to Mateo.

But the boy paid no attention. His little sister was jumping up and down beside him, trying to look in the windows. The boy turned his attention to the poster the Robertsons had put over the CLOSED sign.

"What's this?" the boy said. He pulled on it, and it came away easily. He stared at the sign underneath.

"See?" Pete said. "It's closed."

The boy stood with his hands on his hips, studying the sign. "What do all these words mean?" he asked. "Why does Mr. Santiago have his name on this?"

Mateo had finished selling the oranges to the Romeros and he and Mr. and Mrs. Romero came over to the table. Jupiter had walked toward Pete and the children.

"Miguel, Angela," Mrs. Romero called. "Come over here."

The boy didn't move.

"Do you know him?" Jupiter asked the boy. "Mr. Santiago?"

The boy turned and nodded. "He's our neighbor. He lives down the street. I thought he worked for you."

"For who?" Pete said. "You mean, for the Robertsons?"

"Miguel," Mr. Romero said sternly. "Mind your mother."

Reluctantly Miguel came over. He had a wide, open face and a bowl haircut. His sister bounced at his side, grinning. Pete could see she'd recently lost a tooth.

"Why did you say you thought Mr. Santiago worked for us?" Mateo asked him.

Miguel looked uncertain and shook his head.

"We can't tell you," Angela said. "It's a secret."

"What kind of secret?" Pete asked.

"He told us not to tell," Miguel said. "He wanted it to be a surprise."

"He wanted to make you grow really big oranges!" Angela said.

Mateo turned to Mr. and Mrs. Romero. "Do you know what they're talking about?" he asked.

"No idea," Mrs. Romero said. "The things kids make up."

"Did you make this up?" Mr. Romero asked Miguel.

"No, papi," Miguel said.

"Then tell Mateo what you mean."

Miguel seemed shocked that things had become so serious so quickly. "Mr. Santiago said he wanted to give you a Christmas present," he said, "but he wanted it to be a secret. He had a special magic fertilizer to give to the orange trees so that they would make very big oranges."

"He wanted us to sneak into the middle," Angela said.

"The middle?" Mateo asked.

"The middle of the trees," Miguel said. "He gave us these tubes and he wanted us to bury them in the ground by the trees. Then they would do their magic. Did it work?"

"He said we could dress up as magic elves if we wanted!" Angela said, jumping up and down.

Miguel shook his head. "Stupid," he said. "No elves. But he drove us out here and we planted the magic fertilizer. He gave us each an ice cream cone."

Pete looked around him. Everyone stood silently, expressions of amazement, shock, and anger on their faces. Mr. and Mrs. Romero clearly couldn't believe their children had gotten involved in something like this, and Jupiter looked absolutely stunned. It was really astounding how trusting and gullible children could be, and how sweet it was that Angela had been so excited about being an elf. And it was also horrible to use them like that.

"Don't tell Mr. Santiago we told you!" Angela said. Her glee had turned to distress at the reaction of the adults. "We promised!"

It all made sense now. The fertilizer tubes that his aunt and uncle had found were not old; they'd been planted last winter by the Romero children, and they'd contained no magic fertilizer but rather salt that had poisoned the trees.

Mr. Romero looked at Mateo and opened his hands as if to say, *What is going on?*

"This is the first I've heard of any of this," he said. "I hope the kids didn't do anything wrong."

Mateo looked like he wanted to get his hands on Arsenio Santiago, but all he said was, "No, Mr. Romero, they didn't do anything wrong. They were just being kids."

Mr. Romero picked up the bag of oranges the family had bought. "Let's go now," he said. "We don't want to hold these good people up."

Mrs. Romero herded Miguel and Angela toward the car. In frustration, she swatted at Miguel's behind. "What were you *thinking*?" she said in a strangled voice.

"Well, that explains that," Mateo said

when they were gone. "The next time that bastard comes by the carnival, he won't know what hit him. I saw the jerk this morning. He may be a tree poisoner, but he seems to take his job as a safety inspector pretty seriously. He was climbing all over The Nemesis, making sure everything's in working order for tonight. He was checking the carts and everything, really carefully."

Pete was having a hard time piecing all this together. When everyone had calmed down, he said, "At least it explains why the orange trees are dying. But just a little while ago we thought the person behind all this was Franklin Weaver! Isn't it?"

"Maybe not," said Jupiter. "I can't believe I forgot to ask Cueball if he was one of the teenagers Charlie Robertson had arrested after the incident in the grove. We can ask him tonight at The Roundup – and if he wasn't one of the three, maybe he knows whether Arsenio Santiago was. After all, the two of them are about the same age, since they both grew up in Bakersfield, it's possible he would know.

"In any case, this is excellent news," Jupiter added to Mateo. "Really wonderful. Because even if it turns out that Arsenio Santiago *isn't* behind the diversion and adulteration of the Robertsons' Remedies packages, once your parents make a report – and with the evidence of the Romero children – the police will *have* to investigate Santiago for salting the orange trees. At that point, someone with a lot more resources than *we* have will be able to find out what's really going on with your supplement."

"I can  hardly wait to tell your folks!" Pete said.

"They're going to be relieved," Jupiter agreed. "As for us, I think the only thing we can do for the rest of the day is what we're already planning to do – go to The Roundup tonight to observe Santiago. It's too bad he's met us already, but after all, the place ought to be crowded and dark, and everyone will be a little drunk."

Mallory had been quiet, Pete had noticed – though she'd been listening hard.

"Actually," she said, "there *is* one other thing we could do this afternoon."

"What's that?" Pete asked.

"Ever since Wally called with his story about Frankie Weaver and his California Ice Company box I've been thinking we should check out the barn again. What if that box the Robertsons found when they replaced the floor in the old barn didn't belong to Charlie Robertson at all? What if it's Frankie Weaver's California Ice Company box that's sitting out in the Robertsons' barn? Maybe there's something inside it that really *is* worth a fortune!"

13

## An Ice Box Disappointment

**O**h, well, thought Mallory, as she looked around the barn one last time before joining the Robertsons in their house. At least I was right that the box *did* belong to Frankie Weaver and not to Charles Robertson.

The moment Wally had said that Frankie Weaver had taunted him by mentioning a California Ice Company box, all Mallory had been able to think about was the box she was closing up again right now. While Jupiter and the others had been dealing with the Romero children, she's been visualizing the graying, splintered wood, the streaks of dirt, the stenciled letters, the comic books, the pulp fiction, the athletic trophies.

Ever since she'd first seen the box, something had been nagging at her. Why would Charlie Robertson have buried a box with his childhood mementos on his own land? The contents of the box might seem pretty silly now, but they wouldn't have seemed silly to him at the time. Normally people kept stuff that had sentimental value close at hand. They didn't go around hiding it away or burying it. Unless, of course, they were kids – or almost kids – who thought they'd be able to dig it up soon, to celebrate the moment they were given an orange grove for their twenty-first birthday!

What had really gotten Mallory thinking, though, were the sports trophies. Wally had said that he and Charlie hadn't much liked sports, and that that was especially true of Charlie. When she had originally looked through the box, she had made a list of everything in it. She'd thought she might be able to research who had won the trophies during those particular years. If it hadn't been Charlie himself, who had it been?

Well, now she knew for sure. Before she and the others had gone into the barn, she had grabbed her laptop, flipped it open, booted it up, and started searching.

She'd typed "Lindsay High School, Lindsay, California" into the search box and when she'd clicked on the link, she'd been taken to a home page awash in red.

At the top was the school mascot, a cardinal, and below that were a number of red boxes – a portal for parents, a link to the Lindsay High dress code, and a prominent one labeled ATHLETICS. Mallory clicked on that.

This part of the site was quite extensive, with a drop-down menu for the various men's and women's teams. At the very bottom, in small red letters, she found a number of links. *Patrons of Lindsay Athletics. Our Winning Records. Sports Heroes of the Past.*

She clicked on the last one.

The page was divided by year and by sport. She scrolled to the years 1938, 1939, and 1940, the years engraved on the trophies. Just as she had hoped, The Most Valuable Player Award on the Lindsay High School Cardinals baseball team in 1939 had been given to Franklin Hayes Weaver II. He also won a medal for wrestling. The box was his – and he had almost certainly buried it on the land he thought he would soon own.

"Well, what are we waiting for?" Pete said. "Let's go see if we missed something!"

With Mateo and Estevan leading the way, the six of them had trooped out to the barn, where Mallory had sat cross-legged as she had before, with everyone else hunched down or standing around her. Carefully, she picked up all the items she'd examined earlier, but this time, rather than flipping through them or merely cataloguing them, she looked more carefully.

She was thumbing through the pages of a crumbling old paperback when something at the bottom of one of the pages caught her eye. Someone had underscored a few lines of text and beside it had doodled in the margin. She looked very closely. The pencil marks were lightly drawn and faded, but in the middle of a thicket of loops and arrows she could make out the letters FW. "Look!" she said, showing the page to Jupiter. "Frankie's initials."

Pete grabbed one of the mystery novels and started looking through it. "Here's another one," he said. "It's like what kids do on the covers of their notebooks."

Mallory found several more examples. There seemed no doubt about it; this had been Frankie Weaver's box. Still, there was really nothing in it that could have persuaded his son Franklin to try and push the Robertsons out of business and off their land. Was it possible the comic books had actually been worth something, even back in 1942?

But no, even if some of them might be valuable now, they couldn't have been back then, Mallory thought. She picked up one of the comic books that hadn't been sold by Pete's uncle. It was one she'd never heard of – *Minute Man*, a skin-tight-suited masked avenger with watches on both arms and a small clock in his forehead. The title read "Minute Man vs. the Ant People. Read the thrilling adventure in which the well-timed hero crushes his puny adversaries!"

Mallory shook her head and set it aside. People had the strangest fantasies, she thought.

Just then, a car turned into the driveway, and then a second one. The first contained Mr. Robertson, and the second one Gabriella and her mother, and in no time at all, Mateo and Estevan were stumbling over themselves to explain to their parents and sister that their troubles might be over – that they now knew who had poisoned the orange trees, and that it shouldn't be long now before they also knew whether the same guy was responsible for diverting the packages and adulterating the Valley fever remedy.

Either way – and just as Jupiter had recognized at once – with the possible connection between the two crimes, either the police or higher-ups at Health and Safety would really *have* to understand that David Robertson hadn't been poisoning his own company's products. Since this was the first Dave Robertson had heard about the diverted packages, he was first very shocked, then very relieved.

It took a while to get the day's story fully out, but when they had, Pete's aunt and uncle fervently thanked The Three Investigators for what they'd managed to uncover – at which point Jupiter  said, completely sincerely, that Pete was the one they should be thanking. If he hadn't been his usual friendly self, and started up a conversation with the Romero children, they would be no further along at all.

Yes, he said, Daman Duwalia might have learned that Franklin Weaver had been an early investor in Tehachapi Biogen, and Mallory might have discovered that Franklin Weaver's grandfather had once owned the parcel of land the Robertsons now owned, but clearly all that information had been leading them in the wrong direction entirely. The fact was, nothing and nothing added up to nothing every time.

And while Mallory thought that might be slightly too strong a statement about what the Three Investigators had accomplished,  she felt so relieved that there had been a break in the case – however accidental – that when Lilliana Robertson invited the four of them to stay for dinner again, she didn't at all mind. In fact, it was fun to be around a lot of happy people cooking and eating good food, and the prospect of returning to Rocky Beach in the morning, leaving the Robertsons to sort the rest of this out, was so agreeable that she didn't feel claustrophobic even once. And the conversation at dinner was actually pretty interesting. Mrs. Robertson was quite heated up.

"All these government agencies," she muttered, shaking her head. "They get filled with people drunk on their power, with no one to hold them accountable. Even if this Arsenio Santiago is just a lunatic and it turns out that he's responsible only for poisoning our trees and not for also poisoning our supplements, I don't think he'd ever have imagined he could get away with it unless he'd been part of a government bureaucracy."

Mr. Robertson nodded. "I've never understood why people have so much faith in health and safety departments, anyway. They just like to be told the government will keep them safe," he said.

"Which it can't and doesn't," said Pete. "Just before my mom told Bob and me what had been going on up here, we saw a teenage kid drop a rope holding a piano in the air. It crashed to the ground and broke, and if the kid's father hadn't pulled a man out of its path, he might have been badly injured – or even killed!"

"That's exactly what I'm saying," said Mr. Robertson. "No government agents are ever going to be able to stop simple human error, but that doesn't keep them from pretending that they can."

"The way they're hurting kids' initiative is what bothers me most," Mrs. Robertson said. "When Dave and I were growing up, no one was hovering over us all the time — and although we've raised our own children the same way, it's hardly the norm any more. Kids need to try things, have ideas, and go after them — the way Jupiter did when he founded The Three Investigators!"

Jupiter looked modest at this comment, but Pete and Bob both beamed. After dinner, Pete's uncle drove the four of them back to Bakersfield and The Oasis, while Mateo took off for his job at the amusement park. Jupiter still wanted to go to The Roundup to try to spy on Arsenio Santiago. Before they said goodbye, Mateo asked whether they wouldn't rather come out to the Carnival and take a ride on The Nemesis.

"I don't think so," Jupiter said. "As I mentioned — "

"Oh. Right," Mateo said. "Anyway, if

you're done early, come on over. I'll be there, and I can let you on for free. It won't be quite as dark as sometimes. There's a three-quarter moon tonight. I like it. You'll still be able to see things."

When Pete's uncle dropped Mallory and the others off at The Oasis, they showered and changed, then walked across the street. There, as they entered the restaurant, Mallory was delighted to see the bikers again. Of course, they'd said they'd be there, but you never knew. When the bikers had suddenly come to the rescue after Daman's near-collision with Franklin Weaver, she'd ended up really enjoying her ride on the back of Rooster's bike.

Although in real life she could never guess in advance just when her wild side would surface, she'd known that she'd enjoy being on the back of someone else's motorcycle – and Rooster had been so polite when he showed her where to sit and what to do to avoid burning her legs on the tailpipe of his Harley, that he had really impressed her.

In any case, since the bikers *were* here, Jupiter would finally have a chance to ask Cueball what he and Mallory had both forgotten to ask – whether he'd been one of the three teenagers Charlie Robertson had caught in the

Golden Globe, and whether Arsenio Santiago had also been there that night.

But when the bikers caught sight of The Three Investigators, they had something else on their minds — the carburetor throttle slide that Cueball had come into the Salvage Yard looking for, and had finally had replaced, just this morning, by his mechanic Skeet. He and Rooster had gone into the shop to get it taken care of, but it seemed that when the four of them were biking back from the Golden Globe, Cueball had heard some of the same strange sounds his carburetor had been making before he had the throttle slide replaced, and right now he was wondering if Skeet had fixed anything at all.

"But why wouldn't he have?" asked Pete.

"Well," said Rooster. "There was a big distraction in the form of a lady who really didn't seem as if she should have been there. I don't know what she was looking for, but she carried it away in a paper bag after talking to Skeet about it for quite a while."

"Why didn't it seem as if she should have been there?" Mallory asked.

Rooster smiled. "Well, she wasn't like you, darlin'."

Although Mallory didn't know what that

meant exactly, she could see it was a compliment.

"No, she sure wasn't," said Cueball. "She seemed to think that Skeet had nothing better to do than to listen to her rattle on about something her husband had asked her to buy for him – something he needed really urgently. I think she may have fried Skeet's brain. But enough about that. That Daman Duwalia guy sure took us by surprise. We didn't know until afterwards that he's the star of those *Time Twist* movies. How do you know him, anyway?"

"We solved a case for him," said Pete. "Well, Jupiter did, really. Which reminds me. Your brother Denny told us that when you were a teenager, you were arrested for getting drunk and eating some oranges in a local orange grove. Was that the orange grove you drove us out to today?"

Cueball stared at Pete.

"You know, it's funny you should ask that. Because it actually *may* have been. It's been a long time since the whole thing happened. Over twenty years. Everything looks pretty different after that much time. Trees get bigger, and buildings get changed. But there *was* something about the place that seemed familiar. My apologies to your aunt and uncle if that *was* the place where I got drunk!" he added. "But the only thing I really remember from that night was the two guys who lured me to my doom."

He chuckled, then looked quite sober. "Actually, one of them died of meningitis when he was only twenty. The other's a middle school teacher here in Bakersfield. So I can't really blame *either* of them any more."

Well, that was that, Mallory thought. Although it had always been unlikely that one of the teenagers who Charlie Robertson had had arrested was Arsenio Santiago, it hadn't been impossible until it actually was. Santiago had been somewhere else that night – and while Mallory could hardly have been happier that they were done with worrying about how to help Pete's aunt and uncle, she still wondered what Santiago's motive for poisoning the orange trees had actually been. It had been a weird case, altogether, Mallory reflected.

Still, right now she simply wanted to dance. Or at least to watch some other people dancing – while Jupiter and the other boys kept an eye out for Arsenio Santiago. Turning to Rooster, she said, "Are you guys sticking around for the line dancing? There's line dancing in Scotland. But I bet American line dancing is pretty different."

"I don't know what the Scottish kind is like, but I can show you what this is, if you want to dance with me," Rooster said.

"I'd love to," Mallory said. "Though the boys and I are really here to spy on this guy who works for the Health and Safety Commission. He's already seen us, so it's going to be hard. I don't know how much I can concentrate on the dancing."

"Can I help with the spying?" Rooster asked. "I'll be happy to help if you want."

"That's nice of you," Mallory said. "Maybe."

When the first strains of a fiddle reached them, Mallory began to feel truly interested in what lay ahead for the rest of the evening. The country western music was very different from the traditional Scottish jigs and reels she knew, and she was looking forward to a different sort of line dancing as well. She stood at the edge of the dance floor, near one of the tables that had been set around the perimeter, and took it all in.

The dance floor wasn't crowded yet, but a grid had begun to form. All the dancers were in two lines – front and back and side to side, like the trees in an orange grove. They stepped forward, stepped back, tapped their feet to the side, swiveled, and the lines reformed. Overhead the little white lights twinkled. The air smelled of sawdust and peanuts. People were wearing snap-buttoned western shirts and jeans and cowboy boots, everyone moving together in synchronized rhythm. It made Mallory giddy just to watch.

The bikers excused themselves, saying they were going to the bar for a beer. Mallory and the boys sat at a table, trying to look inconspicuous. As far as Mallory could see, they were the youngest people there. Jupiter made it clear that he was going to be looking for Arsenio Santiago, not experimenting in yet another form of fancy footwork. Bob nodded and said he'd watch as well, but suddenly Rooster was back. The music had stopped, and the dancers were wandering around, waiting for the next tune.

Then the fiddle started up again. "This one is called 'Joey on the Fiddle,'" he said. "It's an easy one. Come on. I'll teach you."

It was clear the other dancers knew what they were doing, and Mallory, who didn't, hoped she wouldn't make a fool of herself. She stood next to Rooster in a horizontal line and studied the feet of the man in front of her. He took two steps forward, tapped to the side with this left foot twice. He did a little twist and turned so that he was facing right, now in a different line. The pattern repeated, though now it was the right foot that tapped out and back, and after the twist the dancers returned to their original orientation.

It was pretty easy, Mallory thought, but the music was fast, and everyone around her was confident, and just when she thought she had it, the steps changed and peoples' feet were sliding rather than tapping. Rooster was keeping up just fine, but Mallory started laughing. Then she looked up and saw Arsenio Santiago. He and a woman had just entered the Roundup. They stood for a moment, surveying the scene.

"That's him," Mallory said, "the guy we're spying on." She pointed. Just then the dancers twisted and started facing a different direction. Mallory craned her head to keep an eye on Santiago and quickly lost track of the steps.

"I've never seen him before," Rooster said. "But I've seen the woman. Just today. She's the woman I was telling you about. The one who took up so much of Skeet's time and attention that he may have actually put Cueball's own throttle slide back on his carburetor. I said hello to her, so she might remember me. Maybe I can dance with her if they move to swing dancing. I can see if I can find out anything."

"That's a great idea," Mallory said. "Thanks!" She found herself liking Rooster more and more.

When the swing music started and Santiago went back to the bar for another drink, Rooster grabbed his chance. Mallory was impressed with how smooth and charming he was as he sashayed over to the woman and began talking. Soon they were dancing. Rooster twirled the woman out and then back in with a delicate touch that Mallory admired. As they finished that dance and began another, she stood with Jupiter, Pete, and Bob, waiting for Rooster's report. When she saw him grinning as he came across the dance floor, she knew he'd found out something.

"What happened?" Mallory asked.

"I reminded her I'd said hello to her at the shop today. I said it didn't seem like she was used to hanging around in motorcycle shops."

"Where was Santiago while you were talking to her?" Mallory asked.

"He was at the bar for a while, talking to someone he knew. Then he was standing staring at us," Rooster said. "It was only two dances, but she was talkative. She said she'd only gone there to pick up something her husband had ordered. You mean, that little paper bag you had? I asked. You *were* paying attention, she said."

Rooster grinned. It was clear he was enjoying himself.

"What was in the bag? I asked, and she said it was just some metal widget. Still, her husband told her it was going to make them real rich – and she said she liked the sound of that! So I kept kidding her and asking how a metal widget was going to make her rich. What was it anyway? So she described it to me, and it sounded – well, just like a regular old cotter pin, if you want to know the truth."

"A cotter pin?" Pete asked. "You mean one of those metal thingies? With two prongs you pull apart when you put the pin on and it keeps things locked together?"

"Exactly," Rooster said.

"The only thing I know about cotter pins," said Pete, "is that you need them to hook a trailer hitch to a truck. A couple of months ago my father asked me to help him do that, and when we didn't set the cotter pin properly, the trailer broke loose and flipped."

"Did she say anything else?" Mallory asked.

"Yeah," Rooster said. "She told me her husband liked to keep secrets, and when she asked him how this was going to make them rich, he wouldn't tell her. But he said it was part of some plan her husband had started calling Operation Nemesis. Then the music stopped and her husband came over."

"Operation Nemesis!" Mallory said. Between the word "operation" and the word "nemesis," she sure didn't like the sound of that.

## 14

## A Very Wild Ride

By the time it was over, most of the events that followed had burned themselves into Jupiter's brain with remarkable clarity, but when he remembered how close he had come to spending the rest of the evening watching the dancing at The Roundup and then going back to bed at The Oasis, he could hardly believe he had been as inattentive – or mindless – as he'd been for more than thirty minutes.

As Rooster was talking, Jupiter leaned forward, concentrating, trying to make sure he heard what the man was saying over the raucous crowd, the music, the stomping feet. The Roundup seemed to pulsate as the dancers swung their partners or moved up and back in dissolving and reforming lines.

Of course, when Rooster suddenly said "Operation Nemesis," Jupiter *did* think that perhaps he and the other Three Investigators wouldn't be leaving for Rocky Beach the following day, after all. Still his initial assumption was merely that whatever Santiago might be up to that involved his wife buying a cotter pin in a repair shop, it must be a long-term endeavor – though useful information to pass on to the authorities.

Part of the problem was that The Roundup had gotten so loud it made it hard for Jupiter to think, but another part could be laid at the feet of human nature When Pete's aunt and uncle had tried to congratulate him on The Three Investigators' discoveries about Franklin Weaver, he hadn't been lying when he'd told them that Pete was responsible for the one real success they'd had in this case.

No, that had been totally true; he and Bob and Mallory had had nothing to do with the accidental uncovering of the Romero children's elf act. And while Jupiter couldn't quite put his finger on the moment he'd started to wish he had never agreed to look into the Golden Globe's troubles, by the time he'd waved goodbye to Daman Duwalia, he'd decided it was time The Three Investigators called it a day and went back to Rocky Beach.

After all, for all the smoke around Franklin Weaver, there was no fire, and no way to be certain that a fire would ever arrive. While Jupiter would have been abashed if the first case The Three Investigators had ever taken on for one of their own member's families had also proved to be the first case they'd ever failed to disentangle, he'd thought they had reached a dead end. The sudden revelation that Santiago had – very foolishly – done something provably criminal had been a big relief to him, and cemented his determination to be done with the case now and leave it to the authorities.

Still, that was no real excuse for the thirty minutes during which he'd simply sat and watched the dancing. Then all of a sudden – and for no particular reason he could pin down afterwards – he remembered that after the Romero family had left the citrus grove, Mateo had said that the next time Santiago came to the carnival to do an inspection, he wouldn't know what hit him.

He'd said that he'd seen the man that very morning – that he might be a tree poisoner, but he seemed to be taking his job as a safety inspector pretty seriously. According to Mateo, he had been climbing all over The Nemesis, making sure everything was in working order.

"He was checking the carts and everything, really carefully," Mateo had said.

When this memory suddenly floated into Jupiter's mind, he had a sudden sickening insight as to what might be about to happen. He remembered Mateo explaining about the special thrills on the nighttime ride of The Nemesis – how he would brake the carts suddenly, at a predetermined spot, and the riders would feel as though they were about to be catapulted over the side of The Nemesis.

He also finally remembered the cotter pin.

What if, rather than checking the carts for safety, as Mateo had thought he was doing, Arsenio Santiago had been making them *less* safe? Jupiter thought. What if he had messed with the fastenings of the carts – or at least one of the carts? What if he'd placed a cotter pin that might break in the connection between one of the roller coaster's carts and the mechanism that held it fast and started and stopped it?

Why Arsenio Santiago had wanted a new cotter pin – the one he'd had his wife pick up – Jupiter couldn't be certain, but if there was an accident tonight, no doubt Santiago would be one of the first people on the scene, and if he'd put a bad cotter pin in one of the carts that morning, he could easily put a good one back in its place and then claim that nothing had been wrong with the equipment. He'd claim it was human error. And everyone would believe him because, after all, he was the safety inspector. Even if they didn't – because of the evidence of the Romero children, something Santiago could not have anticipated – the so-called "accident" would have already happened.

It was then that Jupiter had finally gathered up the other Three Investigators and the bikers and told them what he was afraid of. The bikers borrowed some extra helmets from acquaintances at the bar, and then the eight of them hurried out into the parking lot.

Outside The Roundup, the western sky still held glimmers of the sunset, but Jupiter could see that night had fallen. The moon was just coming up over the mountains to the east, a three-quarters moon on its way to being full. Out at the carnival, excited teenagers would be queuing up to ride The Nemesis. Mateo would be there, getting everything ready, unaware of the danger. Soon he'd be letting the kids on, two by two, letting them ride and then stopping them at the hairpin turn.

Jupiter couldn't remember when he'd seen Pete and Bob so keyed up, and Mallory was agitated, too. She ended up riding behind Cueball, while Bob rode with Knuckles, Pete with Buzz, and Jupiter with Rooster.

"Here," Rooster said as he positioned himself forward, near the handle bars. "Climb on and put your feet on these footpegs." He flipped them down. "Now keep your legs away from the exhaust pipes 'less you want a wicked burn. And hold on tight. Grab the sides of my leathers. If we start going fast and you feel yourself slipping backwards, don't be afraid to hug me."

Jupiter didn't imagine that happening, but he was grateful for the invitation.

As Rooster kickstarted the bike, it came to rumbling life. He turned the throttle, and the warm burble of the engine vibrated up through the seat. Well, thought Jupiter, he was finally riding a motorcycle – and not just any motorcycle, but a Harley built for the open road. He grabbed hold of the sides of Rooster's leathers as the big man stepped the bike backwards and pointed it in the direction of the road.

The bikers clearly had a set routine. Cueball roared out first, followed by Buzz and Knuckles. Rooster, with Jupiter behind him, was the rear guard. From Jupiter's vantage point he could watch the whole procession, the four of them in single file as they leaned together, running through the streets of Bakersfield.

At first their progress was slowed by the number of cars and the regularity of the traffic lights. When they were stopped by a red light, the men steadied their bikes with their boots on the pavement and revved the throttles, filling the air with rumbling. As they got farther and farther from downtown, they began weaving in and out of traffic, the throaty growl of their engines like some strange conversation they were having with each other. Sound changed as they picked up speed. The cars they passed made a thwap-thwap-thwap like laundry flapping on a line in a stiff breeze.

Jupiter kept his focus forward, but through his face shield he caught glimpses of neon, electric blue and orange, and the white smear of light from overhead street lamps.

The four men stayed in single file as they reached the outskirts of Bakersfield and the commercial buildings became fewer and farther between and small ranch houses huddled next to each other on chain-link-fenced lots, their lights sending a warm yellow glow into the night. A German Shepherd barked and jumped up on a fence as they flew by.

And then they were out in the country, going faster and faster. The land whizzed by, flat and dark. The bikes' headlights cast sharply defined cones of brightness before them. Jupiter saw a jackrabbit leap out from the side of the road and barely escape Cueball's wheels. Amid the sparse traffic, the four bikes took over the right-hand lane in a diamond formation. Cueball rode point, with Knuckles and Buzz fanned out to the sides. Rooster came last, positioned directly behind Cueball. Jupiter could see Mallory and Bob holding tight. Pete was hunched forward intently, as though by sheer will he could make the bike go faster.

Jupiter was astonished at how much he liked riding the bike. He liked the thrust of the bike's engine and the way it threw him backwards, the hum it made as it vibrated up through the seat. He liked the wind whipping by. This was the world coming at you straight. The Flex was comfortable and great for travel, but Jupiter had never before understood the way it came between him and what lay beyond the windows. The Harley had a windscreen, but the air came rushing over it in waves. Overhead the moon was an orange with a bite taken out. At the far edges of the night sky the stars sparkled.

This was the west. He thought about cowboys on their horses, galloping over the plains. They must have felt just like this – even better, with no roads to follow and no gasoline to burn. As Cueball, followed by the others, approached the entrance to the Citrus and Carnival Ranch, Jupiter was glad to see that the lights in the amusement park and on The Nemesis still glowed brightly. That meant the ride hadn't started.

Cueball turned down the gravel drive, followed by the others, and roared toward the opening where the rides were set. The orange trees on either side whipped past. The bikes ahead, in their rush, were throwing up gravel and dust. As they got closer, Jupiter could see the lights begin to blink off. They were almost too late. He felt a rising tide of apprehension start in his lower back and shoot up his spine.

Ahead, Jupiter could see the outlines of several of the rides against the sky. The Ferris wheel loomed darkly and looked like it might tip over and fall to earth with a huge crash. The Scrambler, its arms usually pulsing with neon, now seemed like a giant black spider.

By the time the four bikes broke out of the corridor of orange trees and entered the wide open space where the carnival had been built, the last lights had gone off and The Nemesis had started. Jupiter wanted to yell to Mateo to stop everything and turn the ride off, but he was too far away. The grounds at the bottom of the ride were thronged with teenagers – boys and girls out on a date, groups of friends anticipating a thrill.

The Nemesis wasn't a huge roller coaster – it had been built many years ago, before everything had to be bigger – but Mateo had said the ride made up in terms of sheer fear what it lacked in terms of length. Three carts at a time rode the rails, a ride that lasted only a few minutes, but was filled with steep slopes and wild turns and ever-increasing speed.

At a prearranged point in the ride, high up on the superstructure, as a cart was about to whip around a hairpin turn, Mateo would halt the cart, sending the riders lunging forward, making them feel they were about to become airborne. But if the cart Santiago had tinkered with was out on the tracks, with the cotter pin securing it to the machinery damaged or altered, then who knew what might happen? The strain the sudden halt would put on the pin could snap it, and the cart might really become airborne.

Jupiter felt his heart thumping hard in his chest as the bikes shut down and the eight of them jumped off. The first cart had reached the place where Mateo stopped it dead, and in the three-quarter moon's light, Jupiter could see it stark against the night sky. The teenagers in it screamed their heads off, but they were screams of joy and excitement, not screams of terror. Then the cart came to life again, whipping around the hairpin curve and then plummeting down a steep slope, toward the spot where the riders would get out and Mateo would load two new riders.

Maybe they could get to Mateo before it was too late, Jupiter thought. With him in the lead, the eight of them raced toward a booth at the base of The Nemesis from which Mateo controlled the ride.

But before they could reach him, The Nemesis had jerked to life again, and the second cart reached the hairpin turn. There was an unearthly screeching of metal against metal, a crash, and the sound of high-pitched screaming. This time it was terror behind the screams.

In the light the moon threw, Jupiter could see that the cart had torn loose and was tilting over the edge of the superstructure, off the rails. Two bodies were flailing against their restraints. Jupiter thought he had never heard such anguished yelling. On the ground, the crowd waiting to ride The Nemesis began screaming as well, pointing, jumping up and down.

Mateo had shut the ride off and the garish red safety lights that studded its superstructure flashed on, casting a ghastly glow on the distorted faces of the two teenagers hanging on, as Jupiter could see, for dear life. Mateo flipped another switch, and the carnival's grounds were scalded with the stark white of sodium lights, almost as if a huge flashbulb had gone off.

Jupiter shut his eyes against the intense and sudden glare but the image remained – the two terrified kids hanging there, the pairs in the other two carts stuck in place, yelling. Pete, Mallory, and Bob huddled close, staring upwards in shock.

"Come on, Rooster!" Cueball yelled. "After me." He'd already taken off his helmet. He dropped it and tore off his leathers.

"Can we do something?" Pete asked.

Cueball clapped him on the shoulder. "You sure can. You boys follow us." He turned to Mateo. "Young man," he said. "You got any rope in that shed?"

"Yes, sir," Mateo said. He ducked out of sight and returned with a substantial coil of sturdy nylon rope.

"That'll do," Cueball said. "You should

call the fire department – and tell them to call the police." Cueball  started sprinting toward the Nemesis, Rooster beside him.

"What about Knuckles and Buzz?" Jupiter asked, looking back over his shoulder.

"Knuckles tore his shoulder up in a wipeout and Buzz has a bum knee," Cueball said. "It's just me and Rooster and you three boys. Bob was telling me before that he's had some climbing experience."

That was true. Bob had. And in his own way, so had Pete. This kind of thing was his friends' territory more than it was his, actually. Jupiter felt safer – and also more useful! – thinking. When he and the others reached the scaffolding of the Nemesis, Jupiter tilted his head back and looked up. It was at least a hundred feet to the spot where the cart had come loose. The wooden and metal struts were three ranks deep, to support the track's height.

As he stared upwards, Jupiter remembered the Three Investigators' first case of the summer. At Castello Sereno, they'd been trapped in an upper-floor room in one of the house's towers and he and his friends had had to lower themselves on knotted bedsheets. *That* had given him pause and it had only been twenty-five feet or so. This was four times that.

He swallowed hard. His forehead and hands felt clammy and his throat was dry.

"You O.K., Jupe?" Pete asked, looking a little concerned. "Maybe you should stay on the ground and organize things down here."

Pete knew about Jupiter's fear of heights, but as with any fear, there came a time when you had to face it squarely.

"No," Jupiter said. "I'm fine. I want to help."

Cueball came over and pulled Pete, Bob, and Jupiter close. "O.K.," he said. "Here's the plan. Me and Rooster will go first; you three follow. When we get there, I'll sneak up on the track and check things out. We really won't know what we're facing until we look it in the eye. But my guess is we've got to secure that damn cart before we even try to get the kids out. Rooster and I will do the heavy lifting then. Ready?"

Bob nodded, and Pete's face was shining with anticipation. He liked few things better than action. Jupiter nodded his assent at Cueball, trying to look as resolute as possible.

"Good men," Cueball said, slapping their shoulders.

He turned to the wooden scaffolding and started climbing, Rooster beside him. Jupiter was shocked by their speed and agility.

"Lean in!" Cueball yelled up to the kids in the precariously tilting cart. "Stay still."

If Jupiter had been prescient, if he had known ahead of time that he'd be climbing a complicated interlocking structure of wood and steel, he'd have brought leather gloves and worn better shoes – boots, preferably, with deep treads. But all he had were his hands and the shoes he'd put on that morning, with slick leather soles.

The bikers were much better prepared for this. Their hands were calloused and hardened, and they were wearing their motorcycle boots. Just for a moment he wondered if Pete had been right. Maybe he'd cause more problems than he'd solve.

He looked over at Pete's determined face. Second was rising to the challenge, as he always did.

And so would Jupiter.

The wooden and steel supports were easy to grip. Really, he told himself. This was just like climbing a ladder, which he'd done all his life. Before he knew it, he was thirty, forty feet up. Then he made the mistake of looking down.

The ground seemed unfathomably far

away and it swam a bit under his gaze. He felt slightly sick to his stomach. His hands tightened into fists, grasping the scaffolding. His right leg started twitching rapidly, jerking up and down wildly.

He remembered Bob and Mallory talking about rock climbing and this thing called sewing-machine leg. They'd both said it could happen any time, to anyone -- a result of tension, stress, fear. It was automatic, maybe even autonomic, muscle twitches that made your leg tremble uncontrollably.

But if you calmed your mind you could stop it.

Jupiter looked squarely in front of him, at the reassuring solidity of wooden beams and steel supports, at bolts and angle joints, materials from the material world where things stayed put and did not shake. He would not look down again, he thought. He would look straight ahead.

He was involved in a rescue – he did not need rescuing himself. He was fine. He was Jupiter Jones, the First Investigator, and he had a responsibility not only to the teenagers above him but to Pete, Bob, and Mallory. As well as to himself. His leg stopped trembling.

Below him the crowd had quieted as everyone stared up at the five figures climbing toward the precariously balanced cart. The only sounds Jupiter heard were the occasional screams of the kids on the coaster and shouts of encouragement from below. He wasn't sure, but he thought he could pick out Mallory's voice.

He started climbing faster, gaining on the bikers, and he wasn't more than fifteen feet behind Bob when the sole of his shoe slipped on a patch of oil or grease. He caught himself, but not before he'd banged his elbow. The pain was sharp, immediate. For a moment he thought he was losing his balance.

Next to him, about ten feet away, Pete looked at him in alarm. But after the sewing-machine leg, Jupiter knew what to do. He closed his eyes and took a deep breath, told himself that now was no time to give in to pain. He planted his two feet solidly and waited for the pain to lessen. Which it did. He opened his eyes and grinned at Pete.

Cueball and Rooster had reached the top, and Bob, Pete, and Jupiter were right behind them. Cueball slipped under the dangerously twisted railing against which the cart leaned, careful  not to touch either the railing or the cart. He turned and gestured to his companions to do as he had done.

Jupiter held his breath as he passed through the hole in the railing. He felt as if he were threading a needle. The two teenagers were huddled on the interior side of the cart. Jupiter had never seen two people who looked so frightened and miserable.

"Easy now," Cueball said to the pair. "Don't move. This thing is tippy."

Rooster, Pete, Bob, and Jupiter stood next to him now on the wooden slats between the rails, staring for a moment at the chain that had hauled the cart up the lift hill.

What to do? How to proceed? Everyone could see that a false move might result in disaster. The situation looked like one of those puzzle games with blocks or sticks where the whole edifice would collapse in a heap unless you pulled the perfect piece out perfectly. Jupiter, Bob, and Pete all looked to Cueball for instructions. He was a grown man who worked with his hands, who understood the physical world, who knew that if you pushed or pulled, something had to give.

By now, he'd crossed his arms on his chest and was surveying the scene. The silver cross that hung from his ear glinted in the sodium lights. His tone was calm and matter-of-fact as he handed Bob the rope. "You need to get down on your back and snake your way under the cart. There's got to be a grommet or a bracket you can pass it through. Careful not to touch the cart."

Jupiter watched as Bob took an end of the rope and carefully lowered himself onto his back. He inched under the cart's hanging wheels and stared at the undercarriage.

"I've got something," he called out.

"Aces," Cueball said. "Careful now."

Less than a minute later, Bob wiggled back out.

"O.K.," Cueball said. "Now let's get cracking.

The plan was for him and Rooster to take the two ends of the rope and to triangulate the cart, wrapping the ends around steel struts supporting the interior rail both in front of and behind the cart. Then they'd try to steady the cart with their upper-body strength as Pete, Bob, and Jupiter helped the two kids to safety.

When the rope had been tied off, it seemed to Jupiter that the cart was at least halfway secure. Rooster and Cueball picked their way across the machinery in the floor and positioned themselves at the side of the cart, holding on tight. The kids had long ago unbuckled their safety belts and shoulder straps but quite smartly hadn't tried to climb out. If they had, Jupiter could see, the cart would have plummeted over the railing before they'd gotten to safety – taking them with it.

Now, Bob fell back while Jupiter and Pete took their hands and helped them to safety. Rooster and Cueball were still holding on to the cart which tilted ever more perilously. "Bob," Cueball yelled. "Give us a hand."

Bob rushed to grab the cart – but he hadn't quite reached the bikers when, with a high shriek and a grinding of metal, the cart ripped away from them, the outside railing snapped, and the cart teetered, then fell through the air and smashed to the earth.

Although the police still hadn't gotten there, by now, a fire truck had arrived, and with the aid of its bucket, all the teenagers who'd been on the Nemesis at the time of the accident were carried safely to the ground. So were Cueball, Rooster, Bob, Pete, and Jupiter and while Jupiter had no idea how the others felt, his own relief at stepping into the bucket was immense. It was also great to find Mallory waiting for him on the ground – though he had a task to do more important than talking to her at the moment.

Jupiter had seen some plastic sandwich bags on the counter in Mateo's shack. He took one and walked over to stare at what was left of the shattered cart. Much of the body was in splinters, but the metal coupling that had attached it to the rails was still intact. Jupiter examined it carefully, peering down at it in the blazing white light.

Where was the evidence? If his theory of everything had been correct, and if luck were totally on his side, then...

A feeling of utter relief washed over him. All the tension he'd felt when he was on the Nemesis drained away. Because there it was – the damaged cotter pin.

Using the tail of his shirt to keep his fingerprints off it, he wrenched it loose, put it in the sandwich bag, and sealed it. He hoped the police would be able to find some fragment of fingerprint, or some DNA – something that would prove that Arsenio Santiago had been the one who put the damaged pin in place. Then he made his way back to his friends.

Jupiter was pleased to see that Cueball and Rooster were being approached by the kids who'd been waiting in line for the ride with amazement and awe, and that the bikers seemed to be liking it. And why shouldn't they?

he thought. They had indeed acted heroically −
not giving a moment's consideration to their
own safety as they'd swarmed up the superstructure to rescue the endangered teenagers.
Or maybe they had − maybe, like him, they'd
had second thoughts, fears they'd had to over-
come. But they'd pushed through in any case −
and the teenagers who'd come that evening
had clearly never seen anything like what had
just happened.

To Jupiter it seemed as if they'd grown
so accustomed to life being a ride, where all
that was expected was that they sit back and
enjoy the thrills, that the sight of people taking
action had jolted them back to reality. They
were so used to being passive, to having everything done for them, to inhabiting a world in
which everyone waited for particular, desig-
nated people called "rescuers" to show up, that
they were stunned to be reminded that regular
people could also do the job.

Regular people like Cueball, Jupiter
thought.

"You never know what's going to happen
when you wake up in the morning," Cueball
said, smiling at one of the kids and shaking his
head.

In the distance, Jupiter heard the high

whine of a police siren at last. He charted it as it turned off the highway and onto the gravel drive. It veered into the clearing and skidded to a halt. The siren stopped, but the flashers continued to revolve, throwing beams of red and blue light across the faces of the teenagers.

Jupiter was certainly glad they'd gotten there before Arsenio Santiago, who was undoubtedly already on his way to replace the bad cotter pin with a good one. But Jupiter had outfoxed him. When Santiago went looking, there would be no cotter pin at all.

Jupiter took the plastic bag out of his pocket and got ready to introduce himself to the officers. Then he began walking over to tell them what he knew about a very wild ride.

15

## A Nebulous Nemesis

**F**our days later, Pete was still recovering from the sheer strangeness of the events at the amusement park that night. And not just those events, actually. Everything that had happened over in Bakersfield had had an odd feeling about it – a feeling as if The Three Investigators and Mallory had been swimming upstream and mostly getting nowhere, most of the time.

Of course, when Pete and the others had gotten home, his mother had greeted them like conquering heroes But the truth was that compared to most of their cases, this one had seemed all over the place, and while its ending had been a good one for Pete's aunt and uncle – and maybe most of all, for Mateo! – it actually wasn't totally over yet.

Even so, in Pete's opinion, Jupiter already deserved a medal. Though he, Bob, and Jupiter had all played a role in helping Rooster and Cueball avert disaster, it had been Jupiter alone who had put the pieces together, as he so often did. He had connected the cotter pin and Operation Nemesis. He'd also consulted with the police, and when Arsenio Santiago had shown up at the amusement park in his official capacity – called away from the country western bar where he'd been line dancing with this wife – it was Jupiter who'd suggested he should be kept away from the scene of the accident, because it was highly likely that he was actually responsible for it.

Which was what Pete was saying right now. Pete, Bob, Mallory, and Jupiter were all sitting in HQ2 discussing the case. If you could even call it a case, Pete thought.

Well, of course, it *had* been a case, but not one which The Three Investigators had actually *solved*. Pete's conversation with the Romero children hadn't just been unplanned but unplannable – and ditto for Rooster's encounter with Arsenio  Santiago's wife. In the end, it had been Billy Taylor who had taken one thing and another he had learned over time and woven them together into a plausible narrative.

That was probably why Pete was trying so hard at the moment to make sure Jupiter knew how much he appreciated the role he had played in the rescue on The Nemesis.

"No, no, it's true," he said to him now. "You saved Mateo and the Golden Globe as well as the lives of two teenage kids who just wanted to go on a scary ride," he said.

"Well," Jupiter said. "I certainly didn't do it alone."

"Even so, finding that cotter pin was really something. And when Santiago drove in, ready to blame what had happened on my cousin! Do you remember that look on his face when the police told him to be sure to stick around Bakersfield?"

"He's a pretty good actor," Mallory said. "But we already knew that. He convinced us that he really wanted to help your aunt and uncle!"

"Yeah," Bob said, "but that look of outrage and wounded dignity was really something."

"But behind it," Jupiter said, "you could sense the beginning of panic. Remember Wally saying that all bureaucrats think they're members of one big family, so they stick together? I imagine that as soon as Santiago managed to convince Jason Willard – the guy who interviewed Denny Ackers – that the Robertsons were actually trying to poison their own customers and ruin their own business, he thought he was home free. Wally said that the woman at the California DMV was ready to support some faceless person she'd never met, who lived in Nevada, rather than be sympathetic to Wally when he was standing right in front of her. So Santiago thought he count on Willard.

"Of course, Santiago has never done an honest day's work in his life, but since he hangs out almost exclusively with other bureaucrats, he can hardly imagine another way of life – and up until the last three days, he could hardly imagine being held accountable for anything he did do."

"Or didn't do," said Bob.

"I suppose the police would have been able to get him even if they *didn't* understand his motive," said Mallory. "But it would have driven me crazy if Billy Taylor hadn't remembered what Franklin Weaver had told him about hiring Mateo to run Nemesis Nights. Originally he told us it was because Franklin Weaver had liked Mateo that day he'd stopped in at the Golden Globe. But after the disaster, Billy Taylor suddenly remembered that Weaver had *also* mentioned that it was Santiago who had actually suggested Mateo. That he hadn't liked Billy Taylor's own pick, and had urged Weaver to hire someone he could really trust – someone who was really responsible, like Mateo Robertson!"

"I'm glad we were able to go see Franklin Weaver in the hospital," said Bob. "Because I don't think Weaver ever told Billy Taylor that the reason he offered Mateo $2,000 if he took the job and got through the whole summer without an accident on The Nemesis was *also* because of Santiago. He told *us*, though – and until I heard the tone of his voice when he reported the conversation with Santiago, I wouldn't have believed that a rich and powerful man like Franklin Weaver could actually be scared of a bureaucrat."

"It was scary how scared he sounded," Pete agreed. "And all because Santiago had found some construction code violations in his downtown buildings."

"Weaver would have had to almost tear down his buildings to fix them, if Santiago had demanded it in writing," Jupiter said soberly. "That Health and Safety Commission is truly a menace. It gives men like Santiago, men attracted to power without accountability, the perfect cover to do whatever they want – including blackmailing men like Franklin Weaver!"

"It's a really bad system," agreed Bob. "You'd think that when someone who makes just a normal amount of money at his day job turns out to have millions of dollars in the

bank, someone might start to wonder why –
but all a guy like Santiago has to do is go to
Las Vegas on vacation, pretend he hit the jack-
pot, and that seems to take care of that!"

From where he was sitting, on the floor,
in a beanbag chair, Pete had a very clear view
of the old and battered – and now empty –
Central California Ice Company box they'd
been given by the Robertsons – who had given
its contents to Franklin Weaver.

It was clearly too big to hang on their
memento wall, so they'd decided to keep it
here, in the informal area of HQ2. They were
going to ask Leif and Magnus to fix it up a bit
and put a coat or two of matte polyethylene on
the exterior wood so that it wouldn't get any
more battered than it already was, and so that
they could keep stuff in it.

What stuff, exactly, Pete didn't know yet
– though it wouldn't be sports trophies or
comic books!

"I still think it's amazing that men like
Santiago actually invite bribes," Mallory said.
"I mean, the only other person we've run into
on a case who was blackmailing anyone was
Dina Dotheen, in Auburn, and her motives
were personal, not professional. But the police
in Bakersfield seem to think that Santiago has

been doing this for years – though never quite the way he did it here."

"No," agreed Jupiter. "And although men of his proclivities tend not to be the sharpest tacks in the box, what he did in this case was really pretty clever. Though based on a vast misunderstanding on his part."

"You can say that again," said Pete. "I really felt sorry for Franklin Weaver when he told that part of the story." Pete's uncle had been with them when they'd visited Weaver in the hospital, and although Weaver would probably have recognized them, anyway, from having seen them at the site of the accident, it had been helpful when he learned that Pete was the nephew of his next-door citrus neighbor, and the cousin of Mateo, the boy he had promised to pay $2000 if nothing bad had happened on the Nemesis by the end of the summer.

Of course, what had *really* been helpful had been that Billy Taylor had pieced the story together before the gang had gone to see Weaver. Whatever the reason, once Dave Robertson had started asking him questions, the whole story had poured out.

Both Arsenio Santiago and Franklin Weaver had been investors in the consortium

that had bought The Roundup, and one night
when all the investors were celebrating the con-
clusion of their purchase – celebrating in The
Roundup itself, in a private function – Franklin
Weaver had gotten a lot drunker than he
should have and had ended up telling Santiago
that, a few years before, he had tried to buy
the Golden Globe Citrus Grove from the Robertsons.

He'd also told Santiago that the reason
he'd tried to buy it was that his father, Franklin
II, had been promised the grove by own father
when he turned 21; that in anticipation of
someday owning it, Franklin II had buried a
box in the dirt floor of the barn; that the box
had been filled with his greatest treasures – including comic books and baseball cards.

As Weaver thought he had explained to
Santiago – though maybe he hadn't, since
when you're drunk, a lot of things get foggy –
the offer he'd made to the Robertsons had had
nothing to do with the potential value of the
box of "treasures" – which had probably rotted
a long time ago. His motivation had been a
much broader sort of family feeling – the sense
that if he could buy the land his father lost, that
the thing would have come full circle.

It seemed that Franklin II – Wally's

"Frankie" – had resolved to make a lot of money and buy the land back himself when he could afford it. But Charlie Robertson – his nemesis! – had gotten there first.

Back from the war, he'd taken a job working for the guy who'd bought the land when Frankie's mother sold it, and when Charlie had asked if he could buy a tiny slice of the man's citrus empire, the guy had said, why not? Suddenly Charlie Robertson owned the land where Franklin II had buried his box. And he hadn't wanted to sell it.

In any case, Franklin III *did* remember Santiago grilling him about which comic books, exactly, his father might have had in his collection, and – maybe even more important – which baseball cards might have been deposited in the Ice Company box. Though Weaver had no idea how to answer this question, when Santiago had suggested the names Babe Ruth and Joe DiMaggio, he supposed he might have shrugged and said "Maybe." He really didn't remember.

"With a man like Santiago, that's all it would have taken," Jupiter had said to Weaver. "And having convinced himself that Mr. and Mrs. Robertson's land was worth a fortune, because the comic books and baseball cards that had been worth very little when they'd been buried might now be worth many millions, he set out to drive the Robertsons out of business, and to acquire their land at fire-sale prices. He had made enough money from previous bouts of blackmailing men like yourself, Mr. Weaver, so that he could afford to pay what might still be a considerable  amount for Mr. Robertsons's sixty acres."

Here, Jupiter had stopped, while Franklin Weaver, looking distraught, took a sip of water from a cup next to his hospital bed.

"He used a three-part approach to the problem," Jupiter had continued. "His idea of salting the orange trees was the most primitive and he quickly moved on from it to two other, much better ideas. The first was to use The Roundup as a package-laundering address – one which would let him divert Robertsons' Remedies packages long enough to adulterate the contents of the Valley Fever supplement. The complaints about upset stomachs, etc., would be sufficient to tangle the Robertsons' business up in almost endless red tape – and Santiago's hope was that, in and of itself, that would force the Robertsons into bankruptcy. However, if *that* didn't work, his back-up plan was to arrange for an 'accident' at Franklin

Weaver's Citrus and Carnival Ranch – an accident he could blame the Robertsons' teenage son, Mateo, for.

"As we now understand, Mateo is named on his parents' liability insurance. If he could be plausibly blamed for an accident like the one on The Nemesis, although the Robertsons' insurance company might end up having to pay a large amount of money if there were – for example – a wrongful death suit brought by the parents of a teenager who'd been killed – the insurance company would then terminate their insurance for the Golden Globe and Robertson's Remedies – and it would be somewhere between almost impossible and impossible to ever get insurance again."

That was the part of the story that had really made Pete's head hurt. What *good* was an insurance company, if the moment they had to pay something, they stopped insuring you?

Still, it seemed, from what Pete's aunt and uncle – and also Jupiter's aunt and uncle, later on – had said, it was getting harder and harder for small business owners to get insurance for their businesses. The odds were stacked against them every which way but Sunday – and a man like Arsenio Santiago was ideally situated to take advantage of that. The promised $2000 payment to Mateo if he ran The Nemesis safely all summer had been Santiago's idea of the cherry on the top of the cake – a way for Franklin Weaver to deflect the blame from himself to Mateo after the accident Santiago planned to create.

It really had been a very insidious scheme, Pete thought – and one that might have succeeded if the Romero children hadn't spilled the beans – and/or if Rooster hadn't seen Santagio's wife buying a cotter pin. Of course, even if the Robertsons *had* gone out of business and had to sell their land – and Santiago had bought it – he would have found himself bitterly disappointed when he opened the box.

According to Pete's uncle, although it *had* contained some comic books that had increased in value over the course of almost eighty years, the increase had been relatively modest, and there hadn't been a single baseball card in Frankie's collection – though the right Babe Ruth or Joe DiMaggio might, in fact, have been worth millions!

"Oh, well," Pete said now. "It might have been one of the most confusing cases we ever took on, but at least it ended with the bad guy getting arrested and my aunt and uncle and cousins still owning their business. I do hope we end up getting – I don't know, exactly – more *colorful* cases soon. Or even just end up traveling to some place more exciting than Bakersfield. Not that I mean to insult Bakersfield, or anything, but, well – I don't know – it'll be fun to go to Ojai for Connor and Charlotte's wedding in a couple of weeks."

"It really will," said Mallory – but Bob clapped his hand to his forehead. "Good grief!" he said. "I meant to say this the minute I got here. I just got an e-mail from Hector Sebastian inviting the four of us to visit him and Phillipa Paxton at the ranch where he's been renting a cabin. He offered to buy all four of us round-trip plane tickets to Wyoming, using his frequent flyer miles!"

"You're kidding!" Pete said.

He launched himself out of his beanbag chair, thrust his arms in the air, and jumped in place.

"That's just the kind of thing I meant! And Wyoming! We've never been there! Any of us! Jupe, aren't you excited, too?"

Jupiter tried to look as if he was thinking about the question, but he couldn't really manage it. He shrugged and raised his hands in mock surrender – then smiled broadly.

"Oh, Jeez, this is really great!" Pete said, sitting down again. "I want to go home and tell my dad all about it. So let's find out what Bob is going to call this case! I assume it will be the mystery of the something-or-other nemesis."

"I assume that, too," Bob said, smiling. "But I have to admit that I'm going back and forth between nefarious and nebulous. I'm pretty drawn to nebulous, but I'm not sure what I'd mean by it, exactly."

"Why nefarious, though?" asked Mallory.

"Well, I was talking to Mr. Robertson while we were waiting for Worthington to come pick us up, and he said that he really couldn't understand why so many other people seemed to fall for the government's empty promises so readily. He said that government agencies were really good at convincing the public of what he called the nefarious idea that it can keep people safe from harm, when that's clearly ridiculous."

"Boy, is it ever," said Pete. "In fact, ridiculous might be an understatement in this case." For a moment, the image of a crashing piano flashed through his mind. "But what does nefarious mean, exactly?"

"It just means evil or immoral," said Bob, "but since the word 'nemesis' can mean something dangerous and destructive in addition to referring to an enemy, I can't put 'nefarious' in front of 'nemesis' and have it make sense. I mean, in front of the word 'enemy', 'nefarious' seems just plain redundant."

"I see what you mean," said Mallory. "And I like nebulous a lot better, anyway, for this case. When Isabella and Wally were here in HQ2, I remember you saying that, even then, this case was hard to pin down. Wally didn't agree exactly, but the whole time we were trying to get a handle on what was happening, it seemed incredibly slippery – and having a case seem that slippery makes the case itself a sort of nemesis."

"Yes," Bob said. "When we were up in Bakersfield, I was thinking that when the facts of a case are really disconnected, it makes it hard to make sense of them. Hard to write about them – but also to understand them. You could say that being unable to see which of a set of facts is the most important is a nebulous nemesis for everyone."

"And fear itself – you could call *that* a nebulous nemesis," said Pete. "I mean, I should know. Ever since the day I started running away from Terror Castle, I've been afraid of things I shouldn't have been afraid of. I've learned a lot since then, obviously, but even now if someone tells me that something is haunted – like The Nemesis! – I almost believe them. A lot of the time, that's fine – and after all, the whole point of a ride at an amusement park is to be scared just enough to be happy when it's over – but being afraid a *lot* – and of a lot of different things – isn't good for anyone."

"Pete's right," said Jupiter, nodding. "Being overly fearful and timid is a curse. And it seems that there's something about modern life that is making people more fearful all the time. It's fear that makes so many people believe the obvious absurdity that government commissions can actually protect people.

"One of the things we learned in Bakersfield is that not every 'enemy' is a literal bad guy. Though what was happening to Pete's aunt and uncle *was* caused by an actual bad guy, it was caused, even more, by the organization he worked for. These gigantic government agencies like the DMV and the Health and Safety Commission  tend to attract people who either rubber-stamp other people's bad ideas or come up with bad ideas themselves. Like Mrs. Robertson said, they take away people's healthy initiative. You could say the American government is killing the American dream."

"Wow," said Bob. "What a great way to think about the title! The thing is, this case wasn't just slippery, it was also somehow *boring* – which makes me think that the reason the non-elected part of the government is getting bigger and more powerful all the time is that most people just can't stay *interested* in fighting a gigantic blob."

"And the working classes don't have time to," Jupiter added, nodding. "They're too busy keeping things working. I'm glad Daman's making that movie."

"Me, too," said Pete

They all got up and said goodbye, and soon Pete was walking into his parents' kitchen where his father was pouring a beer into his favorite beer mug. Pete was happy to find his father alone right now – and since that thing Jupiter had said about the working classes was rattling around in his mind a bit, after he told him, quite excitedly, about the invitation to Wyoming, he started to talk with him about his background.

Though he wasn't sure why, exactly, his father's beer mug gave him a place to start. It was a pewter mug with a thick glass bottom and, according to Pete's father, it was the only thing his own father had brought to America.

Before he and Pete's grandmother had immigrated to California, Pete's grandfather had been a poor, illiterate Mexican farmer. In Los Angeles, he'd changed his surname from Crespillo to Crenshaw, and he and his wife had gotten jobs as gardeners. When his eldest son, Martín, Pete's father, had graduated from high school, he had given him the mug as a graduation present.

Pete's grandfather had died when he was very young, but he still had some memories of him. He had been an amazing singer, and a Catholic who sang in his church choir, but he had also believed in the promise of America with what Pete seemed to remember as a ferocious passion.

Now, Pete was suddenly wondering whether his grandfather would think that the America he had come to in the 1960s and the America of today were really different. When he asked his father what *he* thought, his father instantly said, "Really different. Really *really* different," – at which Pete told him about the discussion The Three Investigators and Mallory had just had about the government and the phrase "nebulous nemesis."

"Oh boy," said Pete's father. "I like that. And you can take it from me that your grandfather would have been  appalled by the way the American government  has created a class of people who've never done anything in their whole entire lives but ignore and look down on the taxpayers who are paying their salaries!"

Although  that  was  pretty  depressing, Pete was glad to think that, despite everything, he and his friends had managed to save his mother's sister and her husband from a bureaucrat who had gone completely off the rails. Or rather, who had tried to make sure that someone *else* had gone off the rails, Pete thought, smiling to himself.

He wondered if Bob would stumble upon the same analogy when he wrote up his case notes – then thought that he  should tell him to get out his box of Writer's Dice and add "Villainous Bureaucrat" to the dice that listed possible characters!

# ABOUT THE AUTHORS

## Elizabeth Arthur

Elizabeth was born on November 15, 1953 in New York City. She is the daughter of Robert Arthur, the creator of The Three Investigators series. She was educated at Concord Academy in Concord, Massachusetts, the University of Michigan in Ann Arbor, Michigan, Notre Dame University of Nelson, British Columbia, and the University of Victoria in Victoria, British Columbia.

Before she started working on the New Three Investigators series in December of 2018, Elizabeth spent most of her life writing for adults. *Island Sojourn* – a memoir about building a house on a wilderness island in northern Canada – was published in 1980 by Harper and Row. A second memoir, *Looking For The Klondike Stone*, was published by Knopf in 1992. She is also the author of the novels *Beyond the Mountain, Bad Guys, Binding Spell, Antarctic Navigation,* and *Bring Deeps.*

Elizabeth's writing has received fellowships, grants, and awards from the Bread Loaf Writer's Conference, the Ossabaw Island Project, the Vermont Council on the Arts, and the

Indiana Arts Commission. She twice received fellowships from the National Endowment for the Arts and was the first novelist ever given an Antarctic Artists and Writers Operational Support Grant from the National Science Foundation.

Her novel *Antarctic Navigation* was chosen by the New York *Times* as a Notable Book, received a Critics' Choice Award from the San Francisco *Review of Books*, and was chosen as a Best Book of 1995 by *A Common Reader*. In 1996 the novel received the Ohioana Book Award for Fiction from the Ohioana Library Association.

Elizabeth has also taught creative writing at Miami University in Oxford, Ohio; the University of Cincinnati; and Indiana University/Purdue University of Indianapolis, where she directed the creative writing program. She and Steven Bauer met in 1980 at the Bread Loaf Writer's Conference and have been married since June of 1982.

# Steven Bauer

Steven was born on September 10, 1948 in Newark, New Jersey. He was educated at Hanover Park High School in East Hanover, New Jersey, Trinity College in Hartford, Connecticut, and the University of Massachusetts in Amherst, Massachusetts. In 1970 he received a B.A. with Honors in English from Trinity, and in 1975 he received an M.F.A. in English from the University of Massachusetts.

Steven is the author of three books for young people – *Satyrday*, 1980; *The Strange and Wonderful Tale of Robert McDoodle*, 1999; and *A Cat of a Different Color*, 2000. His book of poems *Daylight Savings* was published by Gibbs Smith in 1989 and won the Peregrine Smith Poetry Prize.

Steven's work has received fellowships from the Bread Loaf Writer's Conference and the Fine Arts Work Center in Provincetown, Massachusetts. In addition, he has been given grants and awards from the American Library Association, the Parents' Choice Foundation, the Ossabaw Island Project, the Massachusetts Arts Council, and the Indiana Arts Commission.

From 1979 to 1982, Steven taught literature and creative writing at Colby College in Waterville, Maine. From 1982 to 2009 he taught at Miami University in Oxford, Ohio where he directed the graduate and undergraduate creative writing programs. In 2010 he established Hollow Tree Literary Services, an independent editing business.